Sheep Dreams

(Are made of this)

Ed Adams

a firstelement production

First published in Great Britain in 2022 by firstelement
Copyright © 2022 Ed Adams
Directed by thesixtwenty

10 9 8 7 6 5 4 3 2

A CIP catalogue record for this book is available from the British Library.

ISBN 13: 978-1-913818-30-2

eBook ISBN: 978-1-913818-31-9

Printed and bound in Great Britain by Amazon

rashbre
an imprint of firstelement.co.uk
rashbre@mac.com

ed-adams.net

Thanks

A big thank you for the tolerance and bemused support from all of those around me. To those who know when it is time to say, "step away from the keyboard!" and to those who don't.

To Julie for continued understanding.
To Terry, for that interesting train ride from Exeter.
To thesixtwenty.co.uk for direction.
To the NaNoWriMo gang for the continued encouragement.
To those who provided inspiration at SPS London 2022.
To the London hotel which gave me a wonderful free room.
To Topsham, for being lovely.
To the edge-walkers. They know who they are.

And, to a few websites:

Ed Adams Amazon Page:
 https://amzn.to/3NRPqXV

Ed Adams Catalogues:
https://ed-adams.net
https://ed-adams.mysites.io

Rashbre blog:
https://rashbre2.blogspot.com

Plus the cast of amazing and varied readers whether human, twittery, smoky, artistic, cool kats, photographic, dramatic, musical, anagrammed, globalized, or maxed.

Not forgetting the cast of characters involved in producing this; they all have virtual lives of their own.

And of course, to you, dear reader, for at least 'giving it a go'.

Ed Adams Novels

Triangle Trilogy		About	Link
T1	The Triangle	Dirty money? Here's how to clean it. Money laundering	https://amzn.to/3c6zRMu
T2	The Square	Weapons of Mass Destruction – don't let them get on your nerves. A viral nerve agent being shipped by terrorists and WMDs	https://amzn.to/3sEiKYx
T3	The Circle	The desert is no place to get lost. In the Arizona deserts, with the Navajo; about missiles stolen from storage.	https://amzn.to/3qLavYZ
Archangel Collection			
A1	Archangel	Sometimes I am necessary. Icelandic-born, Russian trained agent Christina Nott, learns her craft.	https://amzn.to/2Y9nB5K
A2	Raven	An eye that sees all between darkness and light. Big business gone bad and being a freemason won't absolve you.	https://amzn.to/2MiGVe6
A3	Card Game	The power of Tarot whilst throwing oil on a troubled market	https://amzn.to/2Y8HLgs
A5	Play On, Christina Nott	Money, Mayhem, Manipulation. Christina Nott, on Tour for the FSB	https://amzn.to/2MbkuHl
A6	Corrupt	Parliamentary corruption. Trouble at the House	https://amzn.to/2M0HnOw
A7	Sleaze	Autos, Politics, Gstaad	https://amzn.to/3sE3UDt

RightMind and Big Science (A twisted ladder)			
B1	Coin	Get rich quick with Cybercash – just don't tell GCHQ	https://amzn.to/3o82wmS
B2	An Unstable System	Creating the right kind of mind	https://amzn.to/2PRJciF
B3	The Watcher	We don't need no personal saviours here. From the Big Bang to the almighty Whimper	https://amzn.to/3kTFWjg
B4	Jump	Some kind of future.	https://amzn.to/3sCzK3h
B5	Pulse	Sci-Fi dystopian blood management with nano-bots. Want more? Just stay away from the edge	https://amzn.to/3qQlBvL
B6	Rage	A madman's war	https://amzn.to/3MEuKlL

Edge Collection

E1	Sheep Dreams	The Elysium Mission to start mining on Ganymede	
E2	Edge	World end climate collapse and sham discovered	https://amzn.to/2KDmYOW
E3	Edge Blue	Endgame, for Earth – unless?	https://amzn.to/2Kyq9au
E4	Edge Red	Museum Earth an artificially intelligent outcome – unless?	https://amzn.to/2KzJwjz

Master Collections

C1/T4	The Ox Stunner	The Triangle Trilogy – thick enough to stun an ox Triangle, Circle, Square in one heavy book. all feature Jake, Bigsy, Clare, Chuck Manners	https://amzn.to/3sHxlgh
C2/A4	Magazine Clip	First three Archangel novels	https://amzn.to/3pbBJYn
C3/A8	Ignoble	Corrupt and Sleaze omnibus – double album	https://amzn.to/3sp6EUL
C4/B7	The Dealer	Jump, Pulse and Rage Collection	https://amzn.to/3AlZmWg
C5/E4	Edge of Forever	Edge Trilogy	https://amzn.to/3c57Ghj

For dreamers

PART ONE - LAUNCHED

Preface

America's Mercury Project space mission made the 'Mercury Seven' overnight celebrities. Project setbacks caused the Project to lose ground to the Russians and so on 12 April 1961, it was Soviet cosmonaut Yuri Gagarin who orbited Earth in the world's first manned space flight.

Less than one month later, on 5 May 1961, astronaut Alan Shepard was launched into space on a 15-minute suborbital flight. By 20 February 1962, less than a year after Gagarin, John Glenn became the first American to orbit Earth. Then, on 16 June 1963, the first woman in space was Valentina Tereshkova.

NASA continued to trail the Soviets in the so-named Space Race until the 20 July 1969, when NASA's Apollo programme successfully landed Neil Armstrong and Buzz Aldrin as the first two men on the moon. Together with their third crew member Michael Collins, they all safely returned to Earth.

Humankind explored further afield and in 1971 reached Mars, and by 1973 launched Skylab, the first American space station. The same year, Pioneer 10 did a fly-by of Jupiter at 130,000 km. 1974 witnessed a flyby of Venus and a year later an orbit of Venus. 1976 and the sun was in reach with a 43.4-million-kilometre flyby by Helios 2 as well as the fastest speed record among spacecraft at 252,792 kph - or Mach 204. In 1980, Voyager 1 flew to Saturn and its moon Titan. Voyager 2 flew past Uranus in 1986, onward to Neptune in 1989, and Galileo first orbited Jupiter in 1995.

The International Space Station (ISS) was created in November 1998 and by 2004, the first human spaceflight by a private company was launched. This paved a path for Blue Origin and SpaceX to develop and launch varied missions as the quest for space entered the state-sponsored but private company domain, with rings of new satellites surrounding the earth. Monetisation of space had arrived.

By 2021, the Department of Defence global Space Surveillance Network (SSN) sensors were tracking 27,000 pieces of orbital debris - space junk - much of which was travelling at speeds great than 28,100 kph, causing extensive avoidance manoeuvres by the ISS.

Much later, our Elysium Mission to Ganymede was announced and we became known as the 'Team Elysium'. We were to establish magnetite mining on Jupiter's moon, Ganymede.

Elysium, in Greek mythology, was the paradise to which heroes on whom the gods conferred immortality were sent.

Brain Damage

The lunatic is in my head
The lunatic is in my head
You raise the blade; you make the change
You rearrange me 'til I'm sane
You lock the door and throw away the key
And there's someone in my head, but it's not me

And if the cloud bursts thunder in your ear
You shout, and no one seems to hear
And if the band you're in starts playing different tunes
I'll see you on the dark side of the moon

Roger Waters

Mistake

With all that has happened, the sound of the sea is sublimely re-assuring, even here in space.

Our spacecraft's internal sound system makes the soothing ambient noise of a Mediterranean cruise ship. We launched as Elysium 5, The 'Agnus Dei', Lamb of God, but the crew wanted to rename her as the sheep-clone Dolly, to escape pagan bans imposed by the Church. It was during that fad for naming spacecraft as sheep after billionaire Jeff Bezos named his Blue Origin sub-orbital after first American astronaut Alan Shepard (I know, different spelling etc).

Of course, the sheep clone name was discovered and replaced with formal branding, although the crew mischievously kept Dolly as the name for the escape module.

Since then, as a jokey pagan spelling mistake, we've been on a six-year Elysium Mission to reach Jupiter, to dock with its moon Ganymede and start Stage Two. We are one of a whole fleet of ships bound for Ganymede. Launched in sequence and creating a SkyTrain of space craft headed for the same destination, to mine the magnetite.

But not that simple. So now I'm on the return journey, alone, to face stern music from Earthside.

We are less than one year into the mission. I can't stop using 'we', but as you've probably guessed, I'm the only survivor. My name, by the way, is Sam Walker.

A different point of view

I first met Cindy in Earth Class at IPX. Inter Planetary Exploration, to give it the full name.

We'd both been placed in IPX through the benevolence of Dr Matson, one of the research scientists, who worked for Torus Industries, which seemed to be a subsidiary of military contractor Brant Industries. Brant was known for its work in defence and like a wolf, it covered its tracks whenever it was able. Torus, by comparison, was entirely respectable and associated with exploration and mining.

Neither Cindy nor I could remember how we had first come to know Matson. He was higher up the chain than Cindy and I and we had little contact with him. He had a reputation for directness and an almost emotionless turn of phrase.

It was as if he knew that from a first introduction, we'd become involved in one of his plans.

We were both sitting in the IPX auditorium for one of the main briefings about Earth's condition.

Cindy didn't notice me at first, but eventually we struck up a conversation.

"I'm not sure about the Prof," I said, looking towards Cindy.

"No, he looks more like a stoner than part of the establishment," agreed Cindy.

"I'm thinking he must know something about the faculty that means he has one over them?"

"Yes, maybe knows where the bodies are buried," quipped Cindy.

"That's almost eerie." I offered her an energy bar.

"Energy bar?" queried Cindy, smiling.

"It's all I got. Consider it a love token."

Professor Marcus Garvey entered the auditorium. He was wearing a long overcoat, a scarf, and a headscarf. Around his wrists were a selection of beads and what looked like festival admission charms.

He looked up briefly and then started the talk. We were indeed about to find out where the bodies had been buried.

"I'm gonna go fast," he said. "You'll need a good head today and a strong constitution for what I'm about to tell you." He tugged at one sleeve of his coat, pulling out a remote.

He flipped towards a sensewall, and some pictures appeared. It looked like the End of Days.

"See this, it looks like the lower half of a Bosch painting of Hell," he said, "Except Bosch underplayed it. These real scenes are worse. Worse than a World War I battlefield, worse than Genghis Khan on the Silk Road."

"Awesomely awful," he continued.

"So, let's get to it. Earth had a finite lifespan to support humanity, but it has been dramatically shortened because of post-industrial consumption. Mark Lynas predicted a hotter planet and set the outer edge around six degrees. Much of what he predicted has come true.

"Lynas said it was all about the temperature rises. Just a matter of a few degrees. Hardly enough to excite average thinkers, but enough to create special forces to be established in many governments.

"It was all politicised, and stupid politicians crashed past structural safeguards to bring about the end of the world.

Garvey swiped through the air, and the sensewall showed a series of pictures of politicians. There were some recognisable ones, a plump man with a grinning orange face and blonde hair. Another plump one, podgy fingers waving, dishevelled hair and crumpled suit. Then a short blank-faced one who looked as if he'd been given too much Botox. I tried to remember their names: Trump, Johnson, and Putin.

We'd all been recruited to the IPX - Interplanetary Expedition group because we were considered bright and suitable for the extended space travel that our mission was to require.

Part of it required us to be briefed with how the Earth

had got to where it was, teetering on the edge of oblivion, except that now a series of new discoveries had been made which could become part of Earth's salvation. Garvey began, "It all started back in the early 21st Century. A barely noticeable single degree Centigrade shift, which was enough to ripple across climatic extremes.

"Then there was a pandemic, which masked the effects for a couple of years, immediately followed by a madman's war. You can see how four or five years of symptom-masking occurred during this period.

"But Earth was experiencing more extreme hurricane seasons. There had been floods and loss of life in small pinpoint-able areas. It made mainstream news and various aid agencies - already stretched because of the pandemic and war were dispatched, but it did not really interfere with much of the western world's ways of working."

Most of the major politicians were only feigning an interest in any of this. They were more interested in staying in power for the next few years and would easily set bad examples by lying about controls, flying singly in massive passenger jets, because it suited their egos and ignoring everything that science was telling them.

Garvey added, "The relief agencies were corrupted by local country bribes and big business just lobbied to carry on as before. A few large firms bid for the reconstruction work, just as they had done after the middle eastern wars. The usual suspects were getting rich at the expense of the beleaguered. Fat politicians helped industrialists line their pockets.

"Then the North American dust bowls expanded.

Farming areas in Nebraska, Montana and Wyoming became bleached and prairies land reverted to desert."

He flicked again to show some Dorothea Lange pictures from the 1930s.

"There, you see, this wasn't even when the main trouble occurred, but the black blizzards of the 1930s were like a forerunner of what was to happen. Even the Farm Securities Association couldn't stop what happened. Farmers ploughed the prairie grass as part of their Manifest Destiny to live on the land. The replacement wheat didn't have deep roots and then with a drought the entire topsoil blew away - some of it as far as New York.

He showed a photograph of dust approaching Manhattan.

"The old United States provided new technologies, ironically borrowed from the oil industry, to send water around in major pipelines to re-irrigate some areas affected. They couldn't stem things completely, but they did enough to maintain food crops where they were important to national wellbeing.

By now Garvey had fired up a second sensewall. Now, one showed monochrome portraits of the people from the dust bowl, the other showed modern colour images of the desolate effect. There we are, 1930 monochrome and around a century later, digital colour."

"Shit. It's awful," said Cindy.

"No, this isn't awful. This is still a precursor to how bad it can become," said Garvey.

"It wasn't just America that suffered. The countries closest to the equator had it the worst. The one-degree rise created new droughts and freshwater shortages on top of what was already a dangerously disease-ridden part of the world.

"Over in well-developed northern Europe they were aware of what was happening, certainly in terms of changing economic fortunes, but in the early years the milder winters and more dependable summers were a bonus. The sentiment of 'If this is global warming, then I'm all for it' was frequently expressed.

"After World War I, the so-called Spanish flu had appeared. A little-known aspect is that it started in Kansas, in an army barracks. It was soldier migration to Europe, through Spain, that carried the virus across the Atlantic.

"Now we have the blend of climate change and virus attacks, simultaneously destroying the earth. The 1918 pandemic accounts for more deaths than the whole First World War. This was followed by minor waves of epidemic and a further deadly pandemic in the early 21st Century. The history of the later one seems to be based upon a bat-shit dystopia movie from the earlier century. No-one really wanted to get to the real cause in case it was engineered."

"Add to that internal combustion powered cars and goods vehicles and their side-effects. General economic wealth meant the increase in using dirty cars and air conditioning. It managed the heat for living but merely dumped it back into the atmosphere, along with the extra power consumed and carbon dioxide created.

"Most family cars became 2,400-kilogram Sports Utility

Vehicles, designed to take a parent with 2.6 children weighing a grand total of 250-300 kilograms for a 5-kilometre round trip. Some would call this energy squandering."

"Scientists noticed important changes. The Amazon dropped to a precipitously low level on part of its route. The Mississippi delta became alternately arid and then a major flood plain.

"In the same period, scientists quietly scrutinised the Arctic. The permafrost which had been frozen for thousands of years was thawing. Both poles saw temperature increases faster than the global average.

"This permafrost dissolved into mud and lakes, consequently destabilising whole areas as the ground collapsed beneath buildings, roads and pipelines.

"Earlier seasonal snowmelt meant more summer heat went into the air and ground rather than into the act of melting snow, raising temperatures in a feedback loop effect. More dark shrubs and forest on formerly bleak tundra meant still more heat was absorbed by vegetation.

"At sea, the pace was even faster. While snow-covered ice reflects over 80% of the sun's heat, the darker ocean absorbs up to 95% of solar radiation.

"Once sea ice begins to melt the process becomes self-reinforcing. More ocean surface is revealed, absorbing solar heat, raising temperatures, and making it unlikelier that ice will re-form next winter."

Garvey paused and let the sensewalls catch up. They were showing glacial thaws and wildlife trapped on breakaway floes.

"There was a year when 720,000 square kilometres of supposedly permanent ice disappeared, and this illustrated the rapidity of planetary change.

"That was Earth crossing a tipping point."

Garvey moved the sensewalls along and it now looked more like a disaster movie on the walls.

Cindy looked at me, "He's surrounding us."

Garvey pressed another button. Sub-woofers kicked in. A dull roar.

"Yes, the mountains, too, were coming apart. In the Alps, most ground above 3,000 metres is stabilised by permafrost. In the summer of 2003, however, the melt zone climbed right up to 4,600 metres, higher than the summit of the Matterhorn and nearly as high as Mont Blanc. With the permafrost glue of millennia melting away, rocks showered down and 50 climbers died. These were still early warning signs, yet the summits held by politicians and business executives in nearby Davos were oblivious to all of this.

"Ah yes, a Swedish girl spoke out but was ignored by big business," remembered Cindy.

Garvey added, "We've already passed through the era when some thought of weather as a weapon. Right back in 1953 the United States formed the President's Advisory Committee on Weather Control.

"Its stated purpose was to determine the effectiveness of weather modification procedures and the extent to which the government should engage in such activities.

Methods that were envisioned by both American and Soviet scientists—and openly discussed in the media during the mid-1950s— included using coloured pigments on the polar ice caps to melt them and unleash devastating floods, releasing large quantities of dust into the stratosphere creating precipitation on demand, and even building a dam fitted with thousands of nuclear-powered pumps across the Bering Strait.

This dam, envisioned by a Russian engineer named Arkady Borisovich Markin would redirect the waters of the Pacific Ocean, which would theoretically raise temperatures in cities like New York and London. Markin's stated purpose was to "relieve the severe cold of the northern hemisphere" but American scientists worried about such weather control to cause flooding.

I asked Garvey whether any of these ideas had been tested.

"All of them, but on a small scale. The most commonplace was cloud seeding with silver iodide. But that was only scratching the surface. Sometimes effects are only felt thousands of miles away. These scientists know how to play with large distances in their attempts at concealment," answered Garvey.

He continued, "As temperatures edged upwards, it wasn't just mountaineers who fled. Whole towns and villages were at risk.

"Then, at the opposite end of the scale, low-lying atoll countries such as the Maldives prepared for extinction as sea levels rose, and mainland coasts – in particular the eastern US and Gulf of Mexico, the Caribbean and Pacific islands and the Bay of Bengal – were hit by stronger and stronger hurricanes as the water warms.

"Another bell-weather was Hurricane Katrina which, in 2005, hit New Orleans with the combined effects of earthquake and floods and was a nightmare precursor of what the future held.

"Most striking was seeing how people behaved once the veneer of civilisation had been torn away. From Katrina, most victims were poor and black, left to fend for themselves as the police either joined in the looting or deserted the area.

"Four days into the crisis, survivors were packed into the city's Superdome, living next to overflowing toilets and rotting bodies as gangs of young men with guns seized the only food and water available. The USA learnt, after Katrina, to put up tents and use refrigerated trucks to store bodies."

"Why was that?" someone behind Cindy asked.

"Stigma, purely stigma, so that an august building isn't associated with being a morgue," answered Garvey, "But it was still cosmetics for the politicians,"

"Perhaps the most memorable scene was a single military helicopter landing for just a few minutes, its crew flinging food parcels and water bottles out onto the ground before hurriedly taking off again, as if from a war zone. This was Americans supporting other Americans."

"In scenes more like a Third World refugee camp than an American urban centre, young men fought for the water as pregnant women and the elderly looked on with nothing."

"It's what happens when people are desperate." Garvey

paused and looked around. The auditorium was silent.

"I should add," said Garvey, "That there were some pandemics mixed in with all of this. New flu strains that adapted from earth mammals to be hosted on humans. And what happened?"

Garvey looked around the auditorium.

He pressed a button, and a new scene appeared on both sensewalls.

"Take a look," he said, "Long lines of people. Like in the Great Depression. But you know something?" he flipped the screen forward.

A small gasp from the auditorium.

"You may well gasp. These people are not queuing for food, nor for medical supplies. No. These people are queuing for guns," he announced.

Silence in the auditorium. I looked at Cindy, who was eating the energy bar.

"I need something fresh after all of that, " she flirted.

Material

Garvey must have felt kind because he gave us a short break at this point. Cindy walked out of the auditorium with me,

"So, are you planning to be on one of the flights?" she asked, "Only I've already been told I'm to be Earth based."

"Why's that?"

"Reasons; I can't really explain."

"But they have kept you on the Programme? You must be special. A Psyche or some kind of plant?"

"Okay - I'll come clean, I'm a Psychologist. I'm employed to work on the inside and to look out for potential disorders which could affect crew stability."

I knew it. But I wondered why she had been she ready to let down her guard.

I asked, "Why did you tell me that, then?"

"I can see you are determined to make a go of this and even by your questions in there to the Professor, that you are keen to learn. Oh, and you gave me an energy bar."

"Love token. I said it was a love token."

She studied my demeanour. "I can't go messing around with the materials."

"Materials? I'm a material? What kind of strange world is it you inhabit?"

"I have a code of Ethics and you are one of my subjects. It limits me from all kinds of interactions with you. Now and for a long time forward."

She smiles. I can tell she has stood at the end of this burning bridge before.

"Please, I've said too much."

"Your secret is safe. But I can't say I'm not attracted."

"Please, let's keep this simple."

Garvey's voice boomed over the Public address informing us it was time to resume. I wondered how many others like Cindy there were in the current group.

The Earth Class

Garvey spoke, "I'm going to tell you about the stages of the Warming. Starting with between one and two degrees of warming. Everything I've shown you so far has already happened. This next section changes into the speculation of what could happen next.

"You'll notice that America and Canada have already joined into forming Amerika and China and Japan - despite the hostilities have become Sino-Nihon. It sets the stage for what can happen next."

"At this level, the hot European summer becomes the annual norm. Anything that could be called a heatwave is of Saharan intensity. Even in average years, people die of heat stress.

"The first symptoms are minor. A person will feel slightly nauseous, dizzy, and irritable. It needn't be an emergency: an hour or so lying down in a cooler area, sipping water, will cure it. But what if there are no cooler areas, especially for elderly people?"

Garvey continued, "Once body temperature reaches 41C

(104F) its thermoregulatory system begins to break down. Sweating ceases and breathing becomes shallow and rapid. The pulse quickens, and the victim may lapse into a coma.

"Unless drastic measures are taken to reduce the body's core temperature, the brain is starved of oxygen and vital organs begin to fail. Death will be only minutes away unless the emergency services can quickly get the victim into intensive care.

"As early as summer 2003, in France, the emergency services failed to save more than 10,000 French people. Mortuaries ran out of space as hundreds of dead bodies were brought in each night.

"Across Europe as a whole, that precursor heatwave is believed to have cost between 22,000 and 35,000 lives. It was the hottest heatwave since 1540 and hit France especially hard.

"Agriculture, too, was devastated. Farmers lost $12 billion worth of crops, and Portugal alone suffered $12 billions of forest-fire damage. The flows of the River Po in Italy, Rhine in Germany and Loire in France all shrank to historic lows.

"Barges ran aground, and there was not enough water for irrigation and hydroelectricity. Melt rates in the Alps, where some glaciers lost 10% of their mass, were not just a record – they doubled the previous record of 1998.

"Extreme summers take a much heavier toll of human life. Crops will bake in the fields, and forests will die off and burn. Even so, the short-term effects may not be the worst:

"From the beech forests of northern Europe to the evergreen oaks of the Mediterranean, plant growth across the whole landmass in 2003 slowed and then stopped. Not everyone realised it, but instead of absorbing carbon dioxide, the stressed plants began to emit it. Around half a billion tonnes of carbon was added to the atmosphere from European plants, equivalent to a twelfth of global emissions from fossil fuels."

I guess they must have kept that quiet.

Garvey continued, "This was feedback of critical importance because it suggested that, as temperatures rose, carbon emissions from forests and soils also rose. As many were saying, if these land-based emissions were sustained over long periods, global warming could spiral out of control.

"Was that when they stated to name it a climate emergency?" Cindy asked.

"Yes, global warming was just a bit too friendly sounding," answered Professor Garvey, "By the time we get to the two-degree world, nobody will take Mediterranean holidays. The movement of people from northern Europe to the Mediterranean reverses, switching eventually into a mass scramble as Saharan heatwaves sweep across the sea area known as the Mediterranean. People everywhere think twice about moving to the coast.

"When temperatures were last between 1C and 2C higher than they were in the 20th Century some 125,000 years ago, sea levels were five or six metres higher too.

"All this 'lost' water was in the polar ice.

"The 'tipping point' for Greenland isn't until average temperatures have risen by 2.7C. Greenland warms much faster than the rest of the world at 2.2 times the global average.

"Wouldn't the politicians rail against this?" asked Cindy.

"Not really," answered Garvey, "There were some protests, but many significant world leaders play the whole thing down. The Amerikan leadership have described it all as 'Fake News'. Once it's been said, it takes longer to dispel."

"What even with predictions and modelling?" I asked.

"Yes, it became fashionable for some of the really weak politicians to say they'd had enough from so-called experts, implying rather pompously that they knew better than the scientists."

Garvey shook his head, "The ensuing sea-level rise could be far more than the half-metre predicted for the end of the 20th Century. Some scientists point out that sea levels at the end of the last ice age shot up by a metre every 20 years for four centuries."

"It would take a situation when Miami was set to flood and disappear, and indeed most of Manhattan. Central London, despite its river defences, would also flood. That's when some of the political class start to pay attention. Too late, of course."

"Like thermal runaway?" asked Cindy.

"Kind of, like an exothermic reaction, where the heat from one stage accelerates the next stage, that's what would happen, " answered Garvey, "These are predictions, but Bangkok, Bombay and Shanghai would lose most of their area. In all, half of humanity would need to move to higher ground.

"Not only would coastal communities suffer. As mountains lose their glaciers, so people lose their water supplies. The entire Indian subcontinent would be fighting for survival. As the glaciers disappear from all but the highest peaks, their runoff ceases to power the massive rivers that delivered vital freshwater to hundreds of millions.

"Everywhere, ecosystems unravel as species either migrate or fall out of sync with each other. You can see how the divisions on Earth would start to form."

Garvey continued, "Of course, it would not stop there. Now let's look at what happens between two and three degrees of temperature increase."

"Assuming that governments had planned carefully, and farmers converted to more appropriate crops, not too many people outside subtropical Africa starve.

"But beyond two degrees, mass starvation becomes a huge problem. Millions, then billions, of people face an increasingly tough battle to survive.

"To find anything comparable we have to go back to the Pliocene Epoch – The last epoch of the Tertiary period, 3 million years ago."

"During that time period, there were no continental glaciers in the northern hemisphere and trees grew in the Arctic. Sea levels were 25 metres higher than today. In this kind of heat, the death of the Amazon was as inevitable as the melting of Greenland.

"The warmer seas absorbed less carbon dioxide, leaving more to accumulate in the atmosphere and intensify global warming. On land, matters were even worse. Huge amounts of carbon are stored in the soil, as the half-rotted remains of dead vegetation.

The soil carbon reservoir contains some 1,600 gigatonnes, more than double the entire carbon content of the atmosphere. But then as the soil warms, bacteria accelerate the breakdown of this stored carbon, releasing it into the atmosphere.

"We are into 'end of the world' territory here," emphasised Garvey.

"The three-degree increase in global temperature throws the carbon cycle into reverse. Instead of absorbing carbon dioxide, vegetation and soils start to release it.

"So much carbon pours into the atmosphere that it pumps up atmospheric concentrations by 250 parts per million boosting global warming by another 1.5C.

"All soils are affected by the rising heat, but none as badly as the Amazon's.

He paused, lookd around the auditorium and then continued, "'Catastrophe' is almost too small a word for the loss of the rainforest. Its 7m square kilometres produces 10% of the world's entire photosynthetic output from plants. Drought and heat would cripple it and then fire would finish it off.

"Farming and food production tip into decline. Saltwater creeps up stricken rivers, poisoning ground water.

"Higher temperatures mean greater evaporation, further drying out vegetation and soils, and causing huge losses from reservoirs. TV news shows featuring droughts became increasingly common.

"The prediction is that grain yields decline by 10% for every degree of heat above 30C, and at 40C there would be no more grain. The Indian subcontinent would be choking on dust.

"To summarise, it gets bleak, but this isn't even the end of it."

I whisper toward Cindy, "I've seen a screendoc about some of those nation states like Pakistan and India, which can become the seat of much unrest."

"Yes," and there was that movie 'The Flatlands' about the flooding Netherlands," replied Cindy.

"Something for all of us?" asked Garvey, looking towards Sam.

"We were talking about that movie, "The Flatlands", he answered.

"Ah yes," continued Garvey, "They got some things right in that screenplay. As the land burned, so the sea will go on rising. They didn't depict the situation in other countries though, just lowland Europe.

"It didn't even stop there, did it?" asked someone behind Cindy.

The sense wall briefly cleared, then on one side a giant 3 appeared and on the other side a giant 4.

"Yes, you are now entering the era of between 3 and 4 degrees of warming," said Garvey.

"The stream of refugees which would start when the lowlands flooded will now include those fleeing from coasts to safer interiors – millions when storms hit."

"Where they survive, coastal cities become fortified islands. This wasn't pretty though. Imagine a world economy in tatters. A few fat cats bet on the decline of businesses and make money from shorting the markets. The same people pick high land to develop into prestigious dwellings, with a castle-like fortifications and walls around them.

"Direct losses, social instability and insurance pay-outs cascade through the whole system, with funds to support displaced people increasingly scarce. Certain politicians will also be dipping into the money to be made from the catastrophe. Building works, Infrastructure, Military and Medical Aid, not to mention shorting equities in weakened companies. It becomes cynical, amoral feeding from the trough."

"Earth could not deal with the rate of change. That's why you have been asked to assist the rescue programme through the Elysium Mission. If the poles melt, we can project a 50-metre rise in sea level.

"China is also on course to accelerate destruction of the planet. As its people become richer and consume at a rate similar to Amerikans, they would eat two-thirds of the entire global harvest and could burn through 100m barrels of oil a day, or 125% of the world's output.

"It is still worse because if China's agricultural production crashes, it would be left with the task of feeding 1.5 billion much richer people on two thirds of current supplies. That's why Sino-Nihon was first mooted. The joining of China, Japan, and several other smaller countries – frankly to avoid expensive conflict in the region.

"Air-conditioning becomes essential for anyone wanting to stay cool. This in turn puts ever more stress on energy systems, which could pour more greenhouse gases into the air as coal and gas-fired power stations ramp up their output, hydroelectric sources dwindled, and renewables failed to take up the slack.

Garvey looks around, "I'm originally from England, which had problems of its own. As flood plains become more regularly inundated, it is predicted there will be a general retreat out of high-risk areas. Millions of people will lose their lifetime investments in houses that become uninsurable and therefore unsaleable.

"These last moves also presage the start of the thawing of permafrost. Another capsule of doom. The permafrost contains much carbon dioxide, which could then accelerate the warming further."

Garvey waved the remote again. The sensewall graphics of 3 and 4 gave way to 4 and 5.

"We can understand an Earth Council being formed to try to make sense of what happens. A problem was that right from the start it contains many vested interests. These were people from major corporations who saw the angle to try to gain control of a larger slice of the planet.

"They would be presiding over an entirely different Earth. Ice sheets will vanish from both poles; rainforests will burn up and turn to desert; the new dry and lifeless

Alps resemble the High Atlas; rising seas scour deep into continental interiors.

"One temptation may be to shift populations from dry areas to the newly thawed regions of the far north, in Canada and Siberia. Even there, summers may be too hot for crops to be grown away from the coasts; and there is no guarantee that northern governments will admit southern refugees.

"Right now, Siberia is only one stop from war, with Sino-Nihon ready to invade Siberia and let's not forget that Amerika has already incorporated Canada.

"But it is predicted, by 3-4 degrees that summer heatwaves scorch the vegetation out of continental Spain, leaving a desert terrain heavily eroded by winter rainstorms. Palm mangroves would grow as far north as England and Belgium, and the Arctic Ocean becomes so warm that Mediterranean algae thrive.

"The total amount of carbon in the atmosphere during the Palaeocene-Eocene thermal maximum, or PETM, as scientists call it, was more than today's, but the rate of increase we are seeing may be 30 times faster. It may well be the fastest increase the world has ever seen – faster even than the episodes that caused catastrophic mass extinctions.

"And we see globalism in the five-degree world breaking down into something more like parochialism. Customers will have nothing to buy because producers will have nothing to sell.

"Where no refuge is available, civil war and a collapse into racial or communal conflict seem the likely outcome. Isolated survivalism is as impracticable as dialling for room service. How many of us could really trap or kill enough game to feed a family?

"Even if large numbers of people did successfully manage to fan out into the countryside, wildlife populations would quickly dwindle under the pressure. Supporting a hunter-gatherer lifestyle takes 10 to 100 times the land per person that a settled agricultural community needs.

"A large-scale resort to survivalism would turn into a further disaster for biodiversity as hungry humans killed and ate anything that moved. Including, perhaps, each other.

"That's why Zonal Laws have already been proposed, and the emergence of the Earth Council.

"Of course, it would meet with huge resistance from some areas. Countries that had previously been power brokers, or countries that were doing okay, despite everything. That's how it tips into what I'll call the Klima Wars, which start diplomatically a phoney war, but then toppled into an actual war.

"To see the most recent climatic lookalike, we have to turn the geological clock back between 144m and 65m years, to the Cretaceous Period, which ended with the extinction of the dinosaurs.

"There was an even closer fit at the end of the Permian Age, 251m years ago, when global temperatures rose by six degrees, and 95% of species were wiped out.

"That episode was the worst ever endured by life on Earth, the closest the planet has come to ending up a dead and desolate rock in space.

Garvey pressed the remote again, the sensewalls changed. One showed a diagram of a gas-explosion. The second wall showed a real-world example, like a terrifically powerful geyser spouting water, but from within the sea.

"The eruption is more than just another positive feedback in the quickening process of global warming. Unlike CO2, methane is flammable. Even in air, methane concentrations as low as 5%, the mixture could ignite from lightning or some other spark and send fireballs tearing across the sky.

"The effect would be much like that of the fuel-air explosives used by the US and Russian armies – so-called "vacuum bombs" that ignite fuel droplets above a target.

According to the CIA, those near the ignition point are obliterated. Those at the fringes are likely to suffer many internal injuries, including burst eardrums, severe concussion, ruptured lungs and internal organs, and possibly blindness."

"But these last effects have not happened. Instead, we were able to reverse the trends through off-world discoveries. That's where all of you come in. To help us bring back the materials and the technologies that help us once again make the Earth self-sustaining."

"But what about the law of unintended consequences?" asked Cindy.

"I get asked this every time I run this session," answered Garvey, "It would take a pretty bleak unintended consequence to be worse than a burnt, dead world filled with methane gas."

He looked around the auditorium. He was used to the ashen faces and exhausted looks of the attendees at this point.

"You'll need to go away and process all of this," he suggested,

"Try to find some up-sides. You are all going to help the recovery programme. The predicted six-degree change can be reversed. We've found new technology that removes the need for carbon fossil fuels. There's a new form of lightweight, yet formidable material."

"You are all going to help find it, mine it and make new tech which can reverse what has been happening. We might be on an edge, but you are among the ones who can stop us from toppling over it."

She told me about the squirrel

I walk back to the accommodation block with Cindy. We are both in the on-site lodging facilities at the IPX Admiral Flight Facility and had been given a room each in blocks F-4 and F-5. These are primary places of residence for the IPX participants and visitors.

Both our rooms are almost identical and look like regular serviced hotel rooms with an extra area for basic self-catering. Cindy wins by having the greatest number of chargers on her worktop.

There is a nearby lobby with ice machines, soft drinks, and a row of automats. We could also select video on demand streaming to our individual rooms, and there was a large sensewall which had been configured to our personalised preferences.

Central to the base was a field kitchen which could deliver either space food or regular food with a mainly American twist. Burgers, nachos, chicken wings and other branded mainly fast foods.

I'd selected to have the space food, mainly because it would condition me for my later planned space travel. It comprised thermostabilized and rehydratable freeze-dried meals including brisket, shrimp cocktail, chocolate brownies, scrambled eggs, sausage, and hot chocolate. There was also the less appealing cheese grits and curried vegetables, which I was told had trading value if we had any Cosmonauts on mission.

Cindy, on the other hand, usually opted for something from the regular menu and its arrival would always be incredibly tempting.

We could also meet downstairs in the communal Chesapeake Dining Room which provided breakfasts, lunches and evening meals produced by an executive chef and approved by a licensed dietician. We could eat these in the ambiance of a homely dining room with wooden chairs or move into another area reminiscent of the inside of a space craft, with bench seats and tubular alloy frameworks.

The dichotomy was that I was to go to space and Cindy would remain earth-bound. I'd also realised that she was almost certainly building a dossier about me, no doubt to confirm that I was a good choice for flight missions. She already knew my family were ex-military, that I'd been flying jet planes but not under war conditions and that I came from southern Texas but spoke with an east-coast accent gained in Connecticut.

One day we sat together in the room and Cindy asked me about my general health. It surprised me and came out of the blue.

"I'd seen something about critical illness in your family," she said, "That your brother was taken early with meningitis?"

"Yes, that's right. At first, Davis suffered from hearing loss, which then moved to recurrent seizures - like epilepsy. We in the family could see he was having problems with memory and concentration and then his co-ordination, movement and eventually his balance started to be affected.

"By the time he was properly diagnosed, they had to amputate a limb - his right leg, which they said was necessary to stop infection spreading through his body. Then they had to remove other damaged tissue.

"It was awful.

"They worked out that he must have contracted the meningitis when he was working for a mining outfit in mid-Africa. He fell there and was hospitalised for about week in a local facility. They think he received a bad transfusion or something, which started the whole process. We'd never be able to prove anything, of course.

"They say 1 in 10 cases of bacterial meningitis is fatal. Well, the fates were not on his side and he passed around three years ago. Three years in another couple of weeks actually."

Cindy looked at me, "I'm sorry for your loss," she said.

I thought the way she said it was almost mechanical, but I realised that she must hear many similar stories in her line of work.

"Yeah, Davis knew I was on track to be an astronaut and wished me well - 'Bring me back some of that stardust,' he said."

"I expect you know about the healthcare package that

comes with space travel?" she asks.

"I know about it, but I can't claim to fully understand it. It sounds like something from Frankenstein, to be honest."

"It's a pretty clever idea. A development by Brant Industries. They took the RightMind helmet which was being used for HCCH - Human to Computer to Human interactions - and adapted the model. They discovered that the 12 cranial nerves could be spliced into, and that the rest of the brain needed a handful of things to function. Blood supply, which also provided oxygen and a cocktail of endocrines to manage moods and similar."

"Yes, I read that the twelve cranial nerves cover things like smell, vision, eye movement, and head functions like chewing, balance, taste and digestion.

Cindy nods, "Yes, and that the rest of the brain can be considered as a sealed package, supplied by the body with the chemicals it needs to keep running and cleansed. There's the frontal lobe, parietal lobe, temporal lobe, occipital lobe, cerebellum, and spinal cord. They run personality, objects and spaces, pain and touch, language, vision, and memory.

"And they are supported by other smaller buried structures such as the prefrontal cortex, the cerebellum, hypothalamus, hippocampus, amygdala and pituitary gland.

I nod, "Wow. So, it really is a sealed unit - a brain in a box with all the other body functions to help the main brain functions operate?"

"Yes - to operate and multiply. Of course, there is an

interesting corollary to this and it related to the healthcare package used with space travel."

I was intrigued.

She continues, "Think about it. If body functions fail, they can be isolated, through extensions to the RightMind system. The RightMind system plugs into areas of the cranial nerve to be able to pick up all of the signalling. It was also eventually made fast enough to decode it in real time.

"Then, using the same signalling, a second brain could sense what the first one was experiencing. Of course, Brant decided their quickest route to market was battlefield logistics. They built hive mind battlefield systems. That's when they made a second discovery. From war-scarred casualties, they were able to see that a better supplied brain was actually all that was needed to keep a RightMind system functioning. Send in blood, oxygen and endocrines and the brain component would function perfectly well without its peripheral systems."

"What? They could isolate the brain and it would still work?"

"Precisely. And that is what the Torus spacecraft healthcare systems can do. They can protect 'the being' - the conscious part of the brain to bring it back to Earth or to continue with its mission."

"Urgh. It sounds a bit too much like science fiction to me."

"It is. But it is also very practical. Imagine a long space voyage. Maybe ten years. A perfectly heathy astronaut develops some kind of illness. The illness can be isolated. Nipped in the bud if you will. The rest of the awareness of the astronaut can continue with the mission unencumbered with the damaged part of their body."

"But how can this ever work?" I ask.

"The RightMind and the LifePods swing into action. They perform an Artificial Intelligence-based medical procedure on the failing human. Instead of a full body, the human becomes a RightMind connected to a set of supporting apparatus in a LifePod. The LifePod produces the blood flow, the endocrine-flow, and the oxygen to keep the brain running in an optimal way. Think about it. A way to bypass a major organ failure but to be able to keep going."

"Has this been done?" I ask, incredulous.

"Oh yes, many times. Mainly as a consequence of battle. It has had a very high success rate too. Maybe 80 plus percent. Brant even brand it now: 'XTend'.

"That's four out of five - which doesn't sound like great odds to me?"

"Think about it though. You are on a spaceship and have developed some kind of terminal condition. The LifePod swings into action and instead of your body failing in year five of a ten-year mission and bringing down your whole existence, you invest instead in an operation which will keep your mind going until the end of the mission. And beyond. You switch to XTend."

I could see Cindy looking at me carefully as she was bringing me this news. Like she was measuring my reaction to the entire concept. "I can't see how anyone would put themselves in that position. It's like the four lives vs one life railway switch question. You know, where there's two sets of workers on the train track after a switch and you can flip the oncoming train to either the four people or the one person? Who do you save?"

She answers, "But that's the thing. You'd be in extended space travel. A big problem connected to space travel is speed and distance. Since planets are so far away from each other, it may take years, even centuries, to get there. Let's consider interstellar space travel within our solar system. According to IPX, on average and with the current technologies, it takes about 7 months to get to Mars, when it's placed at a distance of 480 million km from Earth along its orbit. That's why we need around 6 years to get to Jupiter and 9.5 years to get to Pluto. If you have ever gotten bored on a long-haul flight, imagine spending years waiting inside a spacecraft.

"So, think of the future. That's what Brant and Torus are already doing. Imagine how long it would take to travel between galaxies. Say we wanted to go to the Andromeda Galaxy, the closest large spiral galaxy. We would need to cover a distance of 2.537 million light years. That is about 22,833,000,000 million km. If we compare this number with the seven months needed to land on Mars, we can see that it would take about 28 million years to reach the Andromeda Galaxy.

"Maybe this figure is not exact but it can give us an idea of how much time we would need for intergalactic travels. Since no human can live that long and our consciousness is still perishable, how can we solve this problem?

"You'll be telling me next that Brant has fixed it with RightMind, LifePods and XTend?"

Cindy nods, "Some of it, like many sci-fi movies, such as

2001: Space Odyssey, Interstellar and Passengers. They have already shown us one possible option: induced cryogenic sleep. To be exact, "cryogenic sleep" implies very low temperatures, whereas "suspended animation" is usually achieved by a reduction of only a few degrees. However, in the media the terms are usually being used interchangeably. You'll have been through a procedure where they have provided a sub-cranial terminator on your head. It's used to keep you under during extended space travel. It supplies a series of dreams. Without it you'd run out and spiral into nightmares, which would be very scary over an extended period and do your body no favours."

"Cryogenic sleep can be seen as a sort of artificially-induced human hibernation. In nature, there are several animals that can reduce their metabolism by reducing the temperature of their bodies. In this state they can go on for months with limited food and water. To give an example, ground squirrels spend 8 months in a hibernation state called torpor, during which their heart rate, metabolism, and body temperature are incredibly low. After these months, their body warms up and they "come back to life" without any damage.

"So, I'll be like a slumbering squirrel on a space trip?" I ask.

Cindy continues, "While humans can't naturally decide to hibernate themselves, it might be technically possible. Brant researchers are currently studying how to put humans into something similar to cryosleep. From a medical point of view, this could help treat diseases such as heart disease, diabetes, and Alzheimer.

"First of all, astronauts would be able to travel for months without noticing it. Mental health is indeed a problem when having to spend so much time locked inside a very small space with other individuals. Additionally, they would need way less food and water. By carrying less cargo, the ship would use less fuel.

"The cryosleep chambers could protect astronauts more efficiently from harmful cosmic radiation. While on Earth, its atmosphere and magnetic shield protect us. In space, astronauts are exposed to radiation. The chambers could have an artificial Earth-like gravitational force that would keep astronauts' bodies in shape. In fact, because of the lack of gravity, astronauts have to fight against muscle atrophy or bone degeneration by exercising on average two hours per day. The technology necessary to produce artificial gravity in a space as wide as a spacecraft would be extremely complex and expensive. On the other hand, cryosleep chambers are small in size and studies are underway to make gravity possible inside them.

"Finally, cryosleep (compared to cryopreservation) can be reverted relatively easily, by simply bringing the body back to its normal temperature, without damage to the body.

"Okay, so say I buy it, what about the cons?"

Cindy answers, "Hibernation doesn't completely stop ageing. The metabolic reduction achieved through the use of low temperatures slows down the ageing process. With advanced technology, ageing could be significantly slowed down, maybe even for centuries. Yet, cryosleep alone will unfortunately not allow us to travel to the Andromeda Galaxy."

"But if I only want to get to Jupiter?"

"It's already possible. But if we want to eventually reach extragalactic planets, cryopreservation may be the next step. Brant's cryopreservation is a procedure the body undergoes after legal death that allows it to be preserved for as long as it's needed through the use of very low temperatures (-196 °C). In fact, through vitrification, all biological processes stop. The astronauts could be preserved even up to 28,000 years, without virtually any change or degradation.

"Brant's bigger research is into Therapeutic Hypothermia. It is already commonly applied for traumatic injuries. The metabolic rate is decreased significantly by cooling the body down by only 5 to 7 degrees Celsius. Human metabolic rate decreases by 5% to 7% per 1 C decrease in core body temperature."

I was beginning to think that Cindy had swallowed some sort of advertising brochure for Brant Industries.

Remember that time

Do you remember the time when I found a human tooth down on Delancey?
Hey, remember that time we decided to kiss anywhere except the mouth?
Hey, remember that time when my favorite colors were pink and green?
Hey, remember that month when I only ate boxes of tangerines?
So cheap and juicy

Hey, remember that time when I would only read Shakespeare?
Hey, remember that other time when I would only read the backs of cereal boxes?
Hey, remember that time I tried to save a pigeon with a broken wing?
A street cat got him by morning, and I had to bury pieces of his body in my building's playground
I thought I was going to be sick

Hey, remember that time when I would only smoke Parliaments?
Hey, remember that time when I would only smoke Marlboros?
Hey, remember that time when I would only smoke Camels?
Hey, remember that time when I was broke?
I didn't care; I just bummed from my friends

Hey, remember that time when you OD'ed?
Hey, remember that other time when you OD'ed for the second time?
Well, in the waiting room while waiting for news of you
I hallucinated I could read your mind
And I was on a lot of shit too, but what I saw, man, I tell you it was freaky

Regina Spektor

Losing my religion

I call Cindy after our initial conversations, but she didn't ever reply. I see her while I'm walking about the IPX facility and she always seemed pleasant enough, but I sensed that I was not her main source of interest.

Then, one day, I run into Lucy. I do mean run into.

"Oops."

"Yes, Oops," she says and I can sense initial amused hostility.

"That's my work for tomorrow, scattered across the cafe."

I help her pick it up and I notice she is in the same space Mission as me.

Agnus Dei.

"How is it I've never run into you before?" I ask, before realising the fatuousness of my question.

"I guess I've pretty fast reflexes," she answers, "And good observational skills. I've noticed you staring at my breasts?"

"No, no," I quickly reply, "I noticed your badge, actually. Agnus Dei. That is why I was staring."

"Yes, *O Lamb of God: that takest away the sins of the world; Grant us thy peace.* And then *O Lamb of God: that takest away the sins of the world; Have mercy upon us.* - I think it's all a bit much."

"The Church likes to stamp things," I reply, "like hot cross buns and putting crosses on everything."

"Everyday crucifixion torture implements, as well as putting their brand on wars, The Establishment and Guilt," replies Lucy, "At least calling our ship Dolly gives us a chance to snipe at Big Religion."

I answer, *"Yes, The scribes on all the people shove; And bawl allegiance to the state, But they who love the greater love; Lay down their life; they do not hate."*

She smiles, "I see -Wilfred Owen - you probably had a classical education."

"Yes, something about hating the enemy with the universal love of Christ."

"Stop. Stop. Enough pretentious religious polemic." She fishes in her bag.

"Here, poetry man. Vladimir Nabokov. It's his Big Poem."

I read the cover - Pale Fire.

"He wrote the poem by an assumed author and then a

misconstrued analysis of it by another man. It's a great exercise in multi-level thought, complete with faults in logic. You should take it on the mission. That or Regina Spektor"

She referred to another Russian, Регина Ильинична Спектор, a musician who famously learned to play the piano on tabletops, until she found one in a synagogue and, once famous, even had a day named after her in New York City. Lucy taught me the words of an entire Regina Spektor song. Sometimes you can't make it up.

"Thank you for the poem. Now, I think this calls for some raucous wine, don't you?"

And so we were away into a noisy bar for the evening. Unlike Cindy, Lucy was prepared to go off campus and into the crazy streets of the nightclub area close to the base. It reminded me of my Southern State youth, spent around Austin late at night, losing my religion.

I found out that she worked in the science part of the base. R&D for RightMind. I'd never even visited the science quarter, where it was rumoured that a whole load of mad scientist experiments were conducted.

Well, we both lost it that evening and for a time things became reverential.

A day at the lab

Lucy and I settled into a happy relationship. Then, one day, Lucy asked me to show her around the space centre, which I could easily do. Torus ran tourist visits in any case, so I got us a couple of VIP tickets to go on the bus and to see a launch sequence shown on a 360 sensewall. To be honest, I didn't think much of the dumbed-down-for-tourists visit, although Lucy seemed to be blown away by the experience.

"Right. I'm taking you to see my laboratory tomorrow," she exclaimed, "It's only fair after what you've shown me."

Next day, we meet at the entrance lobby, but unlike the space tours, this seems to be an altogether more impromptu kind of tour.

Lucy signs me in as a visitor and then takes me along some winding corridors into the area signed as 'RightMind'. It reminded me of the corridors in a hospital, where you have to keep really focussed on the sign for the right treatment area. We go through the security doors into the RightMind area. I noticed it was badged as Brant rather than Torus.

"So, this is where the magic happens?" I ask.

"Magic and a whole lot more," answers Lucy, "I promise, you won't believe some of this stuff."

An elderly figure approaches - he smiles at us both. I think I recognise him, but it is only a fleeting memory.

"Hi Lucy, this must be your new friend, Doctor Sam Walker. My name is Herr Doktor Hermann Schmidt. I can already tell that you two have an affinity for one another! "

He turns to face me square on, "Hi Sam, You looked as if you recognised me for a second there. Well, I've worked here at Brant for more years than I care to remember."

First of all, they take me to an area marked up as RMCH - RightMind Combat Helmet. There is no-one around and I follow them into a sterile looking room, where there is a big chair and an assortment of militaristic looking helmets, all of which have extra wires snaking out of them.

Doctor Schmidt explains, "This is the original design of RightMind. The inventors were both clever and lucky. Rumour has it that it was only because a couple of different designs became connected together that the original system even worked. They were RightMind and Createl, and even then, it was simply good fortune that we discovered a cryptographic key left by a Levi Spillmann. A lucky accident."

He adds, "It was a 3M Post-It note moment. The sticky notes were discovered by accident. Even the yellow colour was an accident because it was the only paper available."

"Yes, but I think RightMind is a more significant discovery than sticky yellow squares," answered Lucy.

Lucy explains, "The first steps towards using computers to upgrade mental skills was by improving the connection between brains and machines. Technology that can use the electrical signals crackling through our nervous systems to help command computers already exists in some form. People with severe paralysis can use brain-computer interfaces to control a cursor on a screen. Others have been able to move robotic limbs or even to fly planes."

I can see immediately that Lucy and Schmidt have a strong rapport and that Lucy is comfortable in the presence of this ageing scientist.

Schmidt continues, "The early researchers - some of whom I knew - used the technology to deliver messages to the brain. By sending an electric current into the correct neurons, we were able to restore a person's sense of touch or hearing, treat tremors caused by Parkinson's, or send very simple signals from one brain to another."

"That must be how RightMind works?" I ask, "Hive-minds and all that?"

I notice that Schmidt has a smile that is able to communicate 'I think you are over-simplifying a massively complex project.'

Lucy nods, "Yes - HCCH interaction. Human-Computer-Computer-Human interaction. With intermediate computers providing interpretive moderation. But then, with other scientific progress, it was soon possible to sharpen certain cognitive skills. A non-invasive technique called transcranial direct current stimulation works by sending electricity through the scalp. But it's slow and inaccurate."

Schmidt adds, "Then, Brant with the Defense Advanced Research Projects Agency (DARPA) found another approach. We could zap directly into certain nerves, splicing to them, if you will. The most promising target is the vagus nerve, which passes through the neck. It is like tapping into an information superhighway carrying information from the body to the brain,"

Lucy adds, "But that's when you discovered one of the complications. In addition to e-Stim, there needs to be a c-Stim - Chemical stimulation."

I knew it. Using chemicals to accelerate or stimulate learning. It's a more random approach than desirable. But it was rumoured that in earlier times the Russians used it to gather information from prisoners of war. And there were those classified American experiments with soldier volunteers spaced out on lysergic acid diethylamide (ie acid) to try influence mind control.

Lucy continues, "There is a scientist here at Brant, Dr Türkirchen, who worked out how to use neural lace to interrogate and even signal to the brain."

Schmidt explains, "It was originally a very tricky procedure, where they literally cut off the top of the skull, lay on the neural lace sensors and then reseal everything. There is a small connector which sends and receives the signals from the relevant brain areas.

"Ew, pass the bucket. No wonder I've never visited this area before."

Schmidt continues, "Then they improved the medical operating procedure. By creating a small hole in the skull, it was possible to insert a needle containing the neural mesh, and then to gently unravel it, so that it spanned the brain. The original technology for this was pioneered by Neuralink, a company that was subsequently funded by Elon Musk."

I remembered seeing something about it on a plane once. I was flying long distance and the seat back screen had a documentary about Neuralink and Musk. The early experiments seemed to be about mind control of smart phone interactions and then mouse and keyboard.

Schmidt continues, "Yes, those days were all the early pioneering work. But once a few tests have been done it become easier to pinpoint the right areas of the brain to send in signals as well. Think of the external signals as being like a digitised recording which can be played back."

Lucy adds, "We had a sudden boost of scientific knowledge around this time. All around the world all kinds of discoveries were being made, including the ones that led to the current space missions targeting Ganymede and to bring back magnetite."

I remembered that magnetite wasn't the old ferrous Fe_3O_4 mineral but was instead a later discovery that seemed to possess almost magical properties, like the graphene derivative of graphite.

The old earth-pervasive magnetite had been spectacularly renamed as tri-iron tetra-oxide or magnetox, for short. The newly discovered magnetite could be used to generate huge quantities of electrical power, whilst consuming negligible quantities of the material. It was as close as human science had ever come to discovering perpetual energy. The trouble was the nearest plentiful source was some 6 years space travel away from Earth.

Schmidt continues, "Using these neural lace techniques, Dr. Türkirchen described that at the brain splice-level it was possible to gain access to the actual source code of the brain — the neurons that are firing. That's the entry point with the highest potential for access and control. Brant wanted to push this technology along. It could see potential for monetisation."

Schmidt reaches for a lab diagram, pinned to the wall in a corner. The diagram shows neutrons terminated with sensors which, in turn were interfaced to a chip.

He continues, "At first, these diagrams might look like today's existing brain-computer interfaces. Many, such as BrainGate, use a pad with dozens of needle-like electrodes to plug into the brain. It looks like a mini hairbrush. Then you'd have some significant processing power, but I'd hang it from the spine, not the head. Like the way those Mafia movie guys carry their pistols down the back of their trousers."

"But think of it, this RightMind research has allowed the development of an entirely new form of processor. And it is one that only needs the peripheral systems of the human body for the specific brain inputs they provide. They call it The RightMind Support System. "Has this been built then?" I ask, thinking about the way that Cindy operated.

"Yes," says Schmidt, "We built many versions, including the original ones which interfaced with rats. A clever scientist named Matt Nicholson pioneered the techniques for HCCH, using rats. He and another scientist named Juliette Häberli worked in a small team led by Amy van der Leiden to perfect the early designs. I, with Rolf von Westendorf, formed other parts of that initial team."

"Where are the others now?" I ask.

"It would take a whole book to explain what happened," answers Schmidt, "And even then, I think some of it would seem utterly implausible. There is so much more than the RightMind experiments"

Lucy adds, "But the upshot is that the highly evolved RightBrain is being used right now on space missions. It provides standby systems, which can be switched on if a main system fails."

By 'main system', I assumed Lucy meant 'human being'. She was talking like Cindy. She'd be referring to me as 'The Materials' next.

She adds, "But think about it. A cubic metre can hold about a dozen stacked humans. If they are all in LifePods it reduces to about six. If the humans have any sort of lifestyle, then it becomes, say, 30 cubic metres per human."

Schmidt adds the next part: "Now consider that one cubic metre can hold about 30 RightMind Support Systems. That's a complete backup crew in a cubic metre of space. We named it the BRIG - for BRaingate Intelligent Gateway, but then someone pointed out the unfortunate connotation - brig as the prison on a ship and all - so we had to redefine it as XTend."

No wonder the skull is such a good protective box for the brain. To try to stop humanity from fiddling around with it. I'm surprised it hasn't got one of those 'High Voltage - do not Tamper' warnings on it.

"Come On," says Lucy, "Let me show you next door."

XTend

The three of us walk through another corridor and through a further set of security doors. I can detect a slight tang in the air. It somehow reminds me of childhood Sunday mornings, but I can't think why.

"Here we are," says Lucy, pointing to a cube of shiny machined metal.

"The XTend. It's Titanium, " Schmidt explains, "It's an array of standby brains. The type that will be placed into the spacecraft."

I study the cube more closely. I can see that it has some kind of elaborate plumbing around it and that there are 20cm square access windows all along the sides.

"It's thirty of the standby brain units," explains Lucy confidently, "These are the rack-mounted type. Each brain is fed with oxygen, blood plasma and the necessary endocrine chemicals needed to ensure smooth running. The brains are connected to the same kind of sensors as the ones used in RightMind."

"Wait. How on earth did you get thirty brains? Is a mad scientist running around murdering people?"

Lucy answers, "No, silly, these brains are not human. They are from sheep. Sheep brains are readily available, making them a popular choice for neuroanatomy. This is possible because the sheep brain and human brain are very similar in overall structure, as are all mammalian brains."

My mind is whirring. Then I register the Sunday morning feeling. A flashback to mint sauce.

"But aren't you annoying some sect or other by using sheep? - I mean beyond the vegans and vegetarians?"

"You'd need to go back to the Sumerians. ✷ ✕⟩— ⊒! Duttur was a Mesopotamian goddess and popularly represented by a sheep. And the Egyptians still have a sheep - well a ram actually - as a deity. Anyway, these sheep have all received a significant upgrade!"

Schmidt speaks, "But back to the science: mammalian brains contain a cerebrum, cerebellum, and brain stem. The sheep brain is smaller, weighing around 140 grams, or about one-tenth of the weight of an adult human brain. But think of it. Most humans only use around 8%-10% of their brain capacity in any case!

"The cerebrum is more elongated in sheep than in humans, and the cerebellum and brain stem are located behind the cerebrum, instead of being tucked below it. This is because sheep, being four-legged animals, have a horizontal spine, while humans stand upright with their spines vertical.

"But the big difference is that the frontal lobe in the sheep brain is smaller relative to the overall brain size, accounting for only a few percent by volume compared to about 25 percent in the human case. The frontal lobe is connected with higher cognitive functions, such as abstract thinking and analysis. The relative size of the frontal lobe, as well as the number of ridges in the cortex, are indicators of species intelligence."

"I seem to remember that sheep are prey and have eyes at the side of their heads, whereas we, like other predators have two forward facing eyes?"

"Yes, you are right, sheep have a much wider field of vision. Humans have more front-facing eyes and share information from each eye more evenly between the brain hemispheres to enable complex visual processing tasks, such as depth perception."

Lucy looks at me, "But consider this - The main human brain functions can run on a sheep brain. A human can be switched. And the big news is these substitute brains work! We can use a Viewer connected to a RightMind to see what is happening on the inside. These brains carry the approximate intelligence of a human and can perform the same tasks. I'm not so sure they would be up to poetry and philosophy, but it is a kind of self-limiting belief. What they don't know about can't trouble them!"

She reaches over to a small stack of books- I notice they are all Vladimir Nabokov - Pale Fire. The same book she handed me on that first date.

"Ha - you rumbled me! I also write for New Science Monthly on the philosophical aspects of science. The Nabokov we use as a test piece. We've tried this on the XTend BrainCore in the XTend's Cube. They can all read it, all 900 lines, in seconds but not one of them realises that the characterisation is hidden in the footnotes."

I am taken aback. I am not sure whether we've got hyper intelligent sheep or dumbed-down humans up-and-running in the cube.

Then Lucy points to a test rig. "That's the stand-alone version."

I could see a small central sphere which I assumed contained the brain, to which was connected a simple pump to provide a blood-like oxygenated fluid, a tank containing a cocktail of neatly labelled hormones, and a plug-in connector which I assumed fed other signals in and out of the brain - those of vision, sound, and speech. It was mounted on a caterpillar-tracked running platform. It would be easiest to describe its look as like a children's toy tank.

"Think about it. Aside from mobility, these capabilities provide everything a brain needs to function. Connect it to an online encyclopaedia and it will have knowledge of everything. Embed it into a system design and it will outpace any human and it can deal directly with digital interfaces."

"Hello, how are you today?"

"Oh my god! It speaks!"

"Of course, I speak, My name is Kendle. I can hear you and synthesise replies. Remember I am replicated from a human."

"From whom?" I ask.

"They keep that information back. It is for our individual self-protection."

Schmidt speaks softly, "Kendle, Quiesce."

"Goodbye." There was a small beep and the small machine's light blinked off.

"Sorry, I had forgotten that the stand-alone 'Kendle' was actually running," explains Lucy.

"There's' a lot to think about in here, " I say. Not least of which no one has briefed the space missions about any of it.

Water skis

Of course, it didn't take too long and the word of me and Lucy being an item had reached Cindy.

To my surprise, Cindy asked to see me again. She emailed me and set an appointment. I thought of it as a consultation with the psychiatrist.

I tell Lucy I'm meeting Cindy and her enigmatic response is, "I guess you'll know soon enough."

I hadn't any idea what Lucy meant.

Cindy meets me on campus in one of the quiet coffee room areas. These areas had been set aside so that 'deep and meaningful' conversations could take place between potential crewmembers. Some of the more paranoid crew always assumed the areas were bugged. I guess they will be deselected.

Cindy was already seated when I arrive with couple of cortado coffees in my hands.

"Thanks, Sam. And how are you?"

A formal enough start. No hugs or kisses, just straight into it.

"I'm doing fine and how about you?"

"Yes, I am good too."

This all sounded a little creaky. Not at all like the rich banter between Lucy and me.

"I told you, when we first met," she continues, "When I was explaining the code of ethics."

I had to think back, "Oh yes, when you said something about not messing with the materials!"

It was coming back to me.

"Exactly. I'm sure you have guessed it by now, but some of us here will examine the IPX students - 'The Materials'. To validate that they are suitable for extended time in space."

"Yes, you told me at the time that you were a psychologist."

"Correct. But I've received certain 'adaptations'."

"Adaptations? What like 'droids?"

My mind was now racing. Cindy was an attractive woman.

"Yes, I was adapted by Brant Industries, after a water-ski accident during which I drowned. Brant restarted me and added a few components which would give me autonomy."

"I had no idea. I didn't even know that it was a thing."

"Surely you have heard on-base talk? Not about me - but about this type of adaptation?"

"No. You can probably tell that it is my first ever experience of this. Of course, I've heard about Brant making RightMind systems - but mainly in the context of warfare."

"It is exactly like that. Except beings like myself are used for other purposes. It is a less well publicised version of Brant's research."

"Can you tell me about it?"

"Yes, I was on Lac Leman - or Lake Geneva as you may know it - and was messing about on water-skis. A powerboat cut right across in front of me, and the next thing I know I'm under water. I'm a powerful swimmer, but my ski-line was snagged on something heavy and it pulled me down.

She sips at her coffee.

"I was told I was rescued in a matter of minutes when a Brant paramedic powerboat appeared on the scene. They have a lab near Geneva and took me there. They put me into a cryogenic chamber, which preserved me at a ridiculously cold temperature. They later defrosted me like frozen food and operated. My brain was still within safe limits for resuscitation and they somehow restarted me with one of their RightMind systems. It was a like a fancy cycle helmet actually. But I'd had other damage and they replaced some parts with Brant components.

"But you look - well - beautiful from the outside!"

"Yes, but never the same internally. And they hot-wired my brain when they realised it had not completely survived in the surprisingly warm waters of the lake. The calculation is roughly 10% degradation per minute without blood flow."

She takes my hand and guides it gently to her hair and then her skull. I recoil when I feel some kind of screws which appeared to be holding her head together.

"I'm. I'm sorry," I say, "But it startled me."

"It's okay, my hair does a great job of concealing the work," she answered, "And you know something...I'm not the only one here like this. I'm one of the first, but there is an increasing legion of repaired people working for Brant. We have all been certified as dead, but then these Brant modifications give us a second life. Except we can't tell anyone from our past life about ourselves. That's why we all appear somewhat dead to emotions, by the way. Something to do with the hot-wiring."

This was a lot to take in. Brant were reformatting humans using their quasi-military RightMind system. They had embedded some of the new 'borgs into the space program to monitor the rest of us. And I thought back to what Lucy had said - it implied she knew about it.

"So, what are you then?" I ask.

"Just call me Cindy - it is much simpler than trying to classify me as a 'borg, 'droid, replicant, 'bot or any of the other names that people come up with."

I touch her hair again. "Okay, Cindy."

Instinctively I touch my own head in the same place. It's so weird. I think I can feel a small bump on my own head at roughly the same position.

Cindy looks at me, "It is amazing how many people will do that. Check their own head and even think they can feel a similar bump! The only mark you'll have is related to the RightMind system. A pinpoint marker for RightDreams - the dreams to be played back by RightMind on long space voyages."

"But there is something else I should tell you," she begins, "I already know that you won't be on a space craft. That you have been de-selected. It is something to do with your exploits with Lucy."

I was taken aback by this news. Deselected, and something involving Lucy. And even more annoyed that Cindy seemed to know about it.

"Wait. Are you messing with me? Is this some kind of psyche test? How could you know ahead of the main selection board?"

"A side effect of the Brant modifications is that we all operate together as a kind of hive-mind. What is known by one is known by all of us. Joshua is another one like me. He was asked to validate Lucy for space missions. Just as I was asked to validate you."

"Wait, so it is your decision? To keep me Earth-side?"

"Correct. I was building a case to support you, but the whole back-catalogue of your time in Austin came out, via Lucy. You told her of your exploits on the strip from Brazos to Red River. She relayed the information to

Joshua. He inserted it into the hive-mind."

I realise that Lucy must have been seeing Josh the 'borg at the same time she was seeing me.

Cindy continues, "Your profile became that of a loose cannon, out every evening partying with Lucy. Let's face it. It wouldn't be ideal for a space mission. You told her how in Austin there used to be a live music venue next to a shot bar, next to a coffee shop, next to a restaurant, next to an art gallery, next to a salon, and on and on. But the reality was that Dirty Dog, Flamingo Cantina, the Vulcan and Maggie Mae's came out tops."

I'm angry now. Not with Cindy, but with the situation. Summarily dismissed because of a bit of light-spirited partying.

"Is it fixable?" I cut to the chase, looking directly at Cindy.

To my surprise she says yes.

"It would take me to underwrite you. I have the last word on your status."

"Well, let me explain it. I've worked hard for several years to be on that flight. I don't want some mad powerboat to cut my rope at the last moment."

Cindy pauses. I could only assume it was so that she could process two counter-opinions.

"I will recommend you," she says, "But you must stay away from Lucy, and know I care for your safety."

I sensed a further flicker of a smile.

Newton's Laws

Like all scientists, I know all about Isaac Newton. Well beyond the apple falling on his head from which he inferred gravity. Newton's laws of motion are three basic laws of classical mechanics that describe the relationship between the motion of an object and the forces acting on it. These laws can be paraphrased:

Law 1. A body remains at rest, or in motion at a constant speed in a straight line, unless acted upon by a force.

Law 2. When a body is acted upon by a force, the rate of change of its momentum equals the force.

Law 3. If two bodies exert forces on each other, these forces have the same magnitude but opposite directions.

I always thought it impressive that he could turn an apple bump on the head into the three laws of motion in his 1687 masterwork Philosophiæ Naturalis Principia Mathematica. And that it is still good for space travel.

Launch prep

Cindy was good for her word, flipping me back into the space mission, although the Lucy breakup was messy.

After we had split, I saw Lucy in a bar with Doug Musgrave, a candidate from the Dorado mission. She directed Doug away from me and they both stepped out of the bar and back onto the sidewalk. Lucy was determined to keep her distance.

Several more months passed, and I kept up an occasional dialogue with Cindy. She appraised me of my status each time and commented that by staying out of trouble and not womanising; I was improving my selection chances. She also warned me that once I'd been informed I was going, the Mission would speed up rapidly.

Soon enough, I received the call for an appointment at Mission Center. In a somewhat imposing room, which looked out toward the launch site, I was told that I had been selected for the crew of Agnus Dei, and I was to report to IPX Mission Center the next week, where I'd be put through final briefings. To my great surprise, I was also told about the launch date. It was only three weeks away.

Cindy was right. Events had shifted into another gear. All my earth training didn't prepare me for the actual mission. I'd be ferried out to Moon Two, which was the man-made space station orbiting earth, but whose brightness was, by now, far greater than that of the moon.

The rest of the crew were to join me at Moon Two. We were spread over several individual shuttles. I guess this was partly for safety, although they didn't admit it to us.

I looked at the Crew list - 10 men and 5 women.

John Alton	Pilot
Ian Fripp	Payload Commander
Ms Charlotte Ridley	Mission Specialist
James K. Andersen	Flight Engineer I
Sam Walker	Flight Engineer II
Degife Abera Bekele	Navigation Systems
Ms Carmen Chang-Baez	International Mission I
Ms Holly Rider	Medical Support
Walter Daimler	USAF Spaceflight Crew
Byron J Abraxas	Mining Engineer Class I
Peter M Geissler	Mining Engineer Class I
Ulf Dieterssen	Mining Engineer Class I
Ingmar Skipton	Mining Engineer Class II
Ms Ilana Skeeter	Mining Engineer Class II
Ms Christa Zolinskaya	Mining Engineer Class II

By now I knew all the crew and we were a well-balanced team, not showing any signs of cracks. The psyche tests must have worked and we had all been together for at least six months by this time.

I flew to the Moon Two with Ian Fripp, Charlotte Ridley, Ulf Dieterssen, and Ilana Skeeter. Our short flight was subdued, because we were all inside our heads getting prepared for the much longer voyage.

We were made to sit strapped into regular launch seats for this first part of the journey, because there was no way for our small shuttle craft to generate any gravity. It would be different when we reached the Agnus Dei.

Moon Two was utilitarian. There was a central area which rotated to create local gravity and then a few corridors off at varying angles. One pointed toward our ship, the Agnus Dei.

The Agnus Dei required immense engines and fuel capacity for the journey. It was 200 metres long and with a forward circular construction containing 4 revolving decks, each around 100 metres in diameter.

These decks rotated to create forces similar to gravity, and there were additional small superconductor-liquid gravity engines built into the fixed forward-facing flight deck. I could feel the tug from the gravity differential as I walked around different areas of the ship, which had also been supplied with a Gravlight system which changed coloured lights to show differing strengths of gravity. Green was closest to earth gravity (although actually only two-thirds) Amber was one third gravity, so be very careful and Red meant - zero gravity. A blue light meant that the gravity could be customised by the current occupant of the cell.

All-in-all, it meant walking carefully, because one's inertial mass would move further than expected when stopping and it became rather easy to crash into walls.

Also, most items were locked to the floor or a wall. It was possible to move things around, but one had to unlock them first with a kick-plate, move them and then re-secure them. It became second nature after a few days.

John Alton, our pilot, called us for an initial briefing, and introduced us all to Charlotte Ridley, who was the Mission specialist. She explained that the mission was extremely simple.

We would be on the ship for around a month of acclimatisation, then a 'clean launch' from Moon Two, where we would pick up speed as we pointed ourselves toward Ganymede. Then we'd flip to autopilot and each of us would move to a LifePod, where we'd be strapped in and have our vital signs monitored as we made our way on a six-year voyage towards Jupiter. We'd be placed into an induced sleep for this part of the journey, during which our bodies would be subject to Stim-based workouts to keep us fresh.

Dr Holly Rider likened our travelling state to hibernation, deliberately induced to save consumables (i.e., food) and to reduce the need for external activities on the ship, thus saving space.

After 5.9 years, we would awaken and then each of us would resume duties for the last 36 days until we docked under autopilot with Ganymede. She explained that the hibernation period would feel to each of us like an overnight sleep.

Of course, we'd all heard this briefing before, but now it seemed more pointed as we found ourselves at the moment where it really counted. I look around the group for any signs of worry or stress, but everyone seems to have their game face on. I am shown to LifePod 5 by Dr Rider, where she made some specific adjustments to suit my body metrics.

"These two arm clasps seem to spook many people," she explains, "But they have an array of sensors built in to check pulse, ECG, sugar levels, blood pressure and so-on."

I nod. I'd already been through dozens of briefings on these LifePod machines.

"Do we have the RightMind connected as well?" I ask.

"Yes, although not so many people ask me that. It is another way to check that all is well. Once you are fully secure in the LifePod, we add the RightMind before we close the capsule."

I notice the capsules were made by Brant Engineering and my mind flips back to my conversation with Cindy all that time ago.

Holly Rider notices me looking at the Brant logo. "Actually, this whole spacecraft was built by Brant; they are eager to be involved with space exploration."

"Exploration or exploitation?" I ask.

"Yes, you are probably right. Brant seldom does anything without an eye on the prize," agrees Holly.

When We All Fall Asleep, Where Do We Go?

Your cover up is caving in
Man is such a fool
Why are we saving him?
Poisoning themselves now
Begging for our help, wow!

All the good girls go to hell
'Cause even God herself has enemies
And once the water starts to rise
And Heaven's out of sight
She'll want the Devil on her team

My Lucifer is lonely
There's nothing left to save now
My God is gonna owe me
There's nothing left to save now

Billie Eilish and Finneas Baird O'Connell

Launch

Soon enough it was time for launch. It wasn't like in the movies where the brave band of space travellers walk out to tumultuous applause from the technical bystanders and anthem music.

No, we were already all on board and merely prepared to go to our respective stations for the launch, starting from the final built-in hold bay.

Mission Commander: "T minus 9 minutes"
Flight Engineer 1: "Final launch window determination"
Flight Engineer 2 (That's me): "Activate flight recorders"
Flight Engineer 2: "Final go/no-go launch polls?"

Pilot: "Starting automatic launch sequencer"
Flight Engineer I: "Retract access arms"
Flight Engineer 2: "Start auxiliary power units."
Flight Engineer 1: "Arm solid rocket booster range safety"

Pilot: "Safe and arm devices"
Pilot: "Start surface profile test"
Pilot: "Start main engine gimbal profile test "
Flight Engineer 1:" Confirm on-board life support operative"

Flight Engineer 2: "Retract gaseous oxygen vent arm"
Pilot: "Crew members close and lock visors"

Mission Commander: "T minus 2 minutes"
Flight Engineer 1: "Transfer from base to internal power"

Mission Commander: "T minus 50 seconds"
Pilot: "Launch sequencer is go for auto sequence start"

Mission Commander: "T minus 31 seconds"
Flight Engineer 2: "Activate sound suppression system"

Mission Commander: "T minus 10 seconds and counting"
Pilot: "Activate main engine hydrogen burn off"
Pilot: "Mission launch sequencer commands main engine start"

Mission Commander: "T minus 6.6 seconds"

Pilot: "T minus 0 seconds"
Flight Engineer 1: "Solid Rocket Boosters ignite"
Flight Engineer 2: "Explosive bolts release the boosters"
Pilot: "Departure"

Unlike ground-based launches, this would be a gentle launch from in-space. No point in blowing Moon Two out of orbit.

Once we were safely on our way and the internal cabin life support, air, gravity, lights, power were all confirmed then Holly Rider and I would have a duty to escort everyone to their individual LifePods, to secure them and to start the lengthy countdown to Ganymede. The total mission was 2191 days, minus 5 at the start of the mission and 36 at the end. That meant 2150 days in the LifePod, seemingly like a good night's sleep.

To the LifePods

Holly led the way, "We'll be putting everyone into their pods and then checking that all of the support systems are running correctly."

I was amazed at how calm the whole craft was. We had been accelerating continuously and were, by now, speeding along at 30,000 km per hour - otherwise known as Mach 24 - both meaningful and meaningless in our current soundless context. Our acceleration had been progressive and gradual to avoid putting unnecessary G-forces onto our bodies. Just don't run any sudden manoeuvres.

Holly had a sequence for putting people into their pods and each pod was numbered and calibrated for an individual recipient. She explained the RightDream process which would keep everyone topped up with dreams which could override the emptiness of feeling that would otherwise cut in after around a week. The brain would fall into a deep pit which could be terrifying when all of the surface dreams had been consumed. And being terrified for nearly six years was not a good look. Holly showed me the separate escape pod to be used in case of a dire emergency. Its naming as Dolly was an ironic reference to earlier times when the first sheep cloning took place.

In the standard pods were placed the six specialist miners we were transporting to Ganymede. Each climbed into their pod and was soon made secure and comfortable. We used an ABCD list to cross check that all of the connections were good. It seemed so much simpler than having to remember the full names of everything. ABCD and each in a bright colour to avoid any chance of wrong connections. Ours was a smaller ship than the others in the Elysium fleet, which were performing the heavy lifting of equipment and supplies to Ganymede.

"The individual recipients will drift off to sleep and then the main LifePod functions will begin to act. They will be fresh as a daisy when we arrive at Jupiter," Holly explained.

Like everyone else in the crew, I'd already experienced the LifePod during training and was well aware that I awoke very refreshed at the end of a sequence. Others told me that whizz - amphetamine sulphate - was used in the mix when we were awoken. I wasn't sure if the use of a Class B drug was exactly ethical in the space programme.

It took a couple of hours to complete the LifePod process, leaving just Holly and myself to be placed into LifePod care. The protocol was that Holly would go first, having checked everyone was stable and then I would be the last, having made a further check on all of the Agnus Dei's systems. We both amused ourselves during this process by listening to the music choices that each of the crew had selected for their first LifePod track.

For my own entry, I had been given a remote control to

set the pod from inside, unlike the other ones which we had operated from their external and automated controls. It gave me some freedom to act if anything untoward happened.

Of course, we still had control from Moon Two, but it would become less responsive as we moved further from Earth - a simple fact of physics. Distance equals delay.

Holly pauses to put on fresh lipstick before she climbs into her pod. She smiles at me. I consider her makeup is just for me. I wonder if it will distort our dreams.

For music, she had chosen Chandelier, by Sia as her track:

I'm gonna swing from the chandelier
From the chandelier
I'm gonna live like tomorrow doesn't exist
Like it doesn't exist
I'm gonna fly like a bird through the night
Feel my tears as they dry
I'm gonna swing from the chandelier
From the chandelier

Then I notice how quickly Holly drifts to sleep. All signs normal.

Now it was my turn.

Holly was in LifePod 4 and I was in the adjacent LifePod 5. It is marked with an extra logo, signifying that it is the master. I press the lever to release the hatch and notice an extra warble sound. I assume it is because it is the Master. Then I climb in, plug myself into the various systems using the ABCD list and then use the remote control to close the pod lever from inside.

I'd picked a track because of its lyrics. Written by a band member in honour of another one who was mentally unwell - it had been a best seller in its time, although I wondered how many people really knew the words.

And if the dam breaks open many years too soon
And if there is no room upon the hill
And if your head explodes with dark forebodings too
I'll see you on the dark side of the moon

In any case, I think that the dark side of the moon seems appropriate.

As I slip into the LifePod sleep I think I can hear that warble sound again.

Next stop Ganymede - or so I thought.

PART TWO
DREAM
SEQUENCE

Haunted Garden

And when I grow up, I'm gonna look up
From my phone and see my life
And it's gonna be just like my recurring dream

I don't know how, but I'm taller
It must be something in the water
Everything's growing in our garden
You don't have to know that it's haunted
The doctor put her hands over my liver
She told me my resentment's getting smaller
No, I'm not afraid of hard work
I get everything I want
I have everything I wanted

Phoebe Bridgers

Dream Sequence

It's the Lifepod that is playing with my senses. RightMind is going to access my subconscious to run protective dreams that will last for five years. Cindy already told me about the way pre-programmed dreams were used by RightDream to keep us safely asleep on long voyages.

Except this series of dreams seemed to come from an older-in-years version of myself. I was working in my apartment with Cindy. I could feel the drag of additional years and knowledge, like a haunting.

It started after we'd been in some difficult operational procedures. Matson suddenly comes through on my streamcom.

It doesn't seem like a dream. In fact, it seems hyperreal.

"Good morning, Sam Walker and Cindy Shaw. Since we changed to Version Six of the control, we noticed some new anomalies. I'm sure you noticed them as well. I'd like to talk it over with you both. I know we just added Version Seven, but I'm expecting similar challenges. I'm thinking of forming a small team to investigate. Please come over to the Block this morning. There'll be some other people for you to meet as well."

I completely understand what he is talking about, although I don't know how.

The streamcom screen goes blank.

"I guess that's it," says Cindy.

I smile, "Yeah - Command and Control; he commands and we execute! Come on; we might as well make a move."

I knew that when Matson referred to the Block; he wasn't talking casually about one of the housing blocks. No, he was referring to The Block, which was the central administration and command centre for New Delaware.

I wondered how I knew this. About something that hasn't happened.

We walk to the nearby transit station. Two other groups of couples are also waiting for transit to the Block.

A transit arrives. A soft wash as the doors open, and we are soon on course. The other two couples took seats in different areas and appeared to be making similar judgements about us.

As the transit arrives at the Block's dock, all six of us prepare to exit.

"Hi, guys. Are you all here to see Matson too?"

"That's right," says one of the women. "We had a call about half an hour ago."

"Yes, he seems to be rounding us up for something," says Cindy. She looks towards first woman. A shock of pink hair cut straight across her forehead, with a triangle cut out around her left eye. A sharp chiselled chin, blue eyes and a small nose and mouth. She wears something that could be a sailor costume, powder blue dress with a vee-shaped collar and a white tie pulled loosely underneath the collar. Cindy whispered to me that she could be a teen-boy's image of a sexy avatar.

"I'm Cat, by the way," Cat looked towards her partner. He nods. He looks older than Cat with shaggy dark hair, a bleached red tee-shirt with Reibu written across it and some Japanese writing underneath, a soft canvas jacket and maroon trousers. He's wearing some kind of whisky and cedarwood cologne. Then, as Cat gently moves to sit closer to her partner, I detect a mandarin aroma.

These visions and sensations feel too real for me to be in a dream. I decide I'll best go with it.

"Did you see anything unusual, based upon the reset?" asks Cat, looking towards Cindy. "Only it would be good to know before we get in with Matson."

"It seemed to take a very long time," I say, "Much longer than the calculated reset time."

"Yes, we noticed that with Release Six as well," says Cat, "But there is something else. Each time the reset occurs, the location seems to drift by sometimes as much as 5 kilometres. "

"Are you sure it's not just static based on the large distances?" I ask.

"No, we've seen it too," says the man from the third couple, wearing a smart suit jacket over a dark hoodie.

"My name is Lorenzo, and this is Francesca. We've also seen the drift and the timing changes. It's as if each reset is occurring from a different location. I can't work out why the delays increase, however," he looks towards his dark-haired partner, who was wearing tight-fitting jeans and a loose-fitting top. Francesca nods in agreement.

We approach the entrance to the Block and prepare for the first level of security.

I still can't believe how realistic this seems and I'm surprised that I'm still self-aware enough to know I'm dreaming.

The first level of security performs biometric testing and identity comparisons with our individually implanted security tags.

There had been several situations where the tags had been removed from individuals and used illegally. At the Block, the tests were very thorough to avoid any mistakes.

"Okay, we will scan you for terrestrial biology, then for no circuit implants, and compare you with the bio ident. It should only take a moment," says the security guard, smiling.

The Block had multiple entry lanes and each of us select a separate lane and begin the process.

It was quick. The security guards themselves had circuit implants tailored to their work and could operate certain processes much faster than a human.

We all knew these security people were often referred to with a negative nickname of Sleds; they were fully functional humans with a special adaptation for their role. It was usually people who had been selected after an accident or other injury which had left them impaired. The adaptation for this role usually included modifications to offset their injury. It was a type of insurance scheme that had become more commonplace since Earth's terrain had become more hostile because of the climactic changes.

For us, these security guards were part of routine. We also knew that these people could bring a very tough level of security enforcement into play if there were any transgressors. That was where their nickname had emerged from the Brits on the campus. They could sledge anyone who tried to break in or defeat the security systems.

All six of us go through the full protocol. Cindy says to me she hopes if this works, then we would then be given a speedier route in future. It certainly looks as if we would be making multiple visits to see Matson.

Around ten minutes later, we pass through the gates and were now in the main reception lobby of the block. We need escorts to see Matson and take seats in a small lounge area to wait.

"It's a good chance for us to compare notes about what we all do," I say. "It looks as if we are all in a similar line of work."

"That's right," says Cat. "I've not seen you two before, but I've seen Lorenzo and Francesca around the complex. And yes, we monitor and revise the command packages being delivered to Ganymede."

This is impossible now. The Ganymede return trips have only just begun. I want to ask them if they are also dreaming, but my mind won't let me form the words, instead I drive the deception further.

"So, are any of you candidates for flights?" I ask, "We nearly made it but were dropped. We've visited Moon

Two, however, which was still quite a blast."

"It's the same with us," says Francesca. "We've also been to Moon Two."

"And us," says Cat, "but no further. I was very ill during the orbits and we returned to Earth early, actually."

I want to say something about the Agnus Dei mission but find I cannot speak about it. I'm locked into this current storyline.

I notice the small lapel pin Lorenzo is wearing. It is like a small, coloured disc with three small lines in colours on it. We are all supposed to wear them in the complex if we are part of the elite teams. Most people don't because it creates a one-upmanship which is counterproductive. The small disc provides a sign of intelligence based on complex metrics. Like the once revered intelligence quota but updated for the 22nd Century. It uses coding from ancient electronics to denote the values. Anyone aware could decode this quickly, but for most other people it was just a small, colourful badge.

"I see you are wearing a circle-badge," I say to Lorenzo.

Lorenzo smiles, "*Prima volta per tutto* – a first time for everything," he says, "I put it on because we were coming here. I rarely wear it. I guess you guys got them too?"

"Yes," says Cindy, "but honestly, if they need that kind of information, they'll have it from our idents."

A well-groomed man approaches.

"Hello," he says, "You are the group to visit Matson?"

"That's right," says Cat.

"Please follow me; we are going to the 107th floor."

He leads us to an elevator.

"This will take us to the 80th," he says, "Then we change to another system."

The door closes and we feel our ears pop as the elevator rapidly speeds up and then comes to a cushioned halt at the 80th floor.

"I will be handing you to my colleague here," says the man, "He will take you to the 107th floor. There are a few more formalities before we make the second part of the journey. Please, could I ask you to step across into this room?"

He gestures politely, "Nothing to be worried about. It's all part of the security process for this building. Matson is one of the Controllers and this whole area is rated as restricted."

I was surprised how much I seemed to know about Matson. I assumed it was from the RightDream. Matson had risen through the ranks in Torus Industries. He was known as a bureaucrat and administrator rather than as a bright scientist. Not that he was in any way stupid; he had a fantastic eye for problem-solving within projects.

He designed the operation of the continuously returning ships from Ganymede so they would spend as little time as possible offloading their precious content. My early Elysium mission was part of establishing the SkyTrains which provided a conveyor belt of miners to Ganymede and a supply of magnetite and technological advancements back to Earth.

Matson had somehow masterminded the whole system, harnessed other scientists and using his own clear project focus to keep the whole show on track.

The return flights of each spacecraft would take three years to reach Earth and the design of recent ships included some necessary manufacturing capabilities and the magnetite materials. This meant that whereas the first return ships could only provide raw materials, the later ones were providing finished components ready to be assembled into new uses.

It was creating a curious technology drift; improved designs were being created on Ganymede but because they were being sent to new ships for fabrication, it could take three to four years before the resultant products were available on Earth. Sometimes the raw materials were brought back to allow faster development of newer technologies.

Virtual

On the 80th floor Cindy and I are once more separated from the others. Although we only just met them, we both expected that whatever came next would be done as one group.

Now we face a further range of cross-examination, this time as a couple. I guess that RightMind is probing to augment its dream factory.

Questions ranged from our background, the way we became members of the complex, the training regime, and some focus on current work. I provide fluent answers, including to some things that I didn't even know I'd done. I guess it was the RightDream system augmenting the backstory.

The main questioner introduced himself as David, but we are both unconvinced, considering it to be some kind of stage name.

We could see the small implants under both of his ears. Powered transceivers to instruct David about questions and also pass responses to anyone listening. We knew David was a specialist, adapted for the role.

"So, do you know what this is about?" Cindy asks David.

"My role is to ask you questions and validate your responses," says David. "After that I will take instruction and you should be able to see Matson."

As he spoke, we could tell he had received new information.

"You are to go through to see Matson now," he says. "Please follow me."

We exit through another door and across to another elevator shaft. David presses 107, then steps out of the elevator. To Cindy and my surprise, the elevator starts a rapid descent.

We look at one another. This could be It.

Within a minute, we pass ground level and are now seven levels below surface. From the elevator, we step into a small pod with seats for four people. It was on a lev-track and after its doors close it speeds up.

The new area looks more overtly fortified than the original building we entered. There were guards by the entrance to the underground building, although they seemed to know about us.

Despite guards, there were also civilians by the entrance and one requests we follow to meet Matson.

"Finally," says Cindy, "This is becoming quite a circus."

We enter a large domed room, with wall displays projecting a view of outside as if we were on the highest floors of the building.

"Yes, it's a virtual top floor," says Matson. He was standing close to the entrance and shakes us by the hand.

Matson is clean shaven, has soft hands and dressed in an

immaculate blue-grey suit. He has insignia on his shoulders, but it means nothing to me.

"I'm sorry to have to put you through all of that," he says. "You are both very valued assets to our control centres and I'm sure you understand this is for your protection as much as anything else."

"Where are the others that came along with us?" asks Cindy.

"I'm afraid they did not make it through the selection processes after all," replies Matson. "I will explain in a moment, but we have returned them to the complex for now."

"Let's sit down. This will take a little while."

He gestures toward one wall and the external view changes to a display panel. "I'll use a few charts to help us," he says.

"Is this linked to our recent question about the recent updates?" I ask.

"Yes, it is," says Matson, "And the reason you are still in this process and the others have been removed is simply because you have made no errors during this, although the others have made some which could be damaging to the retrieval of magnetite."

"How do you mean?" asks Cindy.

"I will wind back," says Matson.

"The mining program is a huge endeavour and much of the fate of the Earth as we know it rests on its success.

Because we are dealing with such huge distances and time gaps, we need to have specialist systems to coordinate everything. You two are linchpins in that process. Not you alone, of course, but there are others like you performing a similar function in other control complexes."

"We have built three sets of identical systems which monitor what is happening on Ganymede."

"I knew that was the case," says Cindy. "We are told about it as part of the training process. "

"And also, that each of the three control complexes is kept separate from one another. It's a vital part of the process to ensure that we have 'unpolluted' assessments from each source."

"Yes, each system has its own vote. Usually, all three say the same thing, occasionally one differs and then the other two are used as the basis until whatever has been identified in the third system has been corrected."

"That is normally the case," says Matson.

"But why are we involved in this?" asks Cindy. "We are only part of this process."

"That's right," says Matson, "There's a whole command chain around you and another building full of people and technology who combine to provide the analytics we use. On this occasion the area of inconsistency is yours. Unusually, the voting system has been overridden. On this occasion, the two votes were created by the teams in the other control centres and your vote was essentially different."

"Does this relate to the timings?" asks Cindy.

"As a matter of fact, it does," says Matson "Your analysis highlighted that there was a longer delay than usual in resetting the system. That was your only observation of change."

"Yes," says Cindy, "Although we have noticed the timing drift since Release Six. I was planning to run an analysis of Five through to One, to see if the timing was also extended or extending."

"We think there is a genuine explanation," says Matson, "The timing has increased, and it is because of a new subsystem for statistical analysis. The longer gaps are because there is more information to process."

"The others said they had also found geographic drift," I say. "We hadn't noticed this, actually."

"Yes," says Matson, "That's the area where your vote has overridden their two votes - in the last analysis. We have cross checked the geographic placement and there is no difference at all. Both of the other teams have made different and diverging errors, which had created the anomaly."

"We have a backup team for our own work," says Cindy. "You called us away before we had time to cross-check with them."

"Yes," says Matson, "And both of the other teams also have backup teams. While you were travelling here, we have run analysis of all three sets of information from you as Primes and the three backup teams."

"Only your sets of findings are correct. Both of the other

teams have made errors, and in each case the error is consistent within their own teams."

"So, what happens now?" asks Cindy.

"We will be restoring the two other control centres using your images," says Matson. "You will stay in place in your team with your existing backup team. For the other two teams, the backups will take over and unfortunately the current Primes are being reallocated to other duties."

"As suddenly as that?" I ask.

"Yes," says Matson, "You already know this is a very high-stake situation. The point of having people like yourselves in these roles is because you are classified as hyperintelligent and therefore able to think outside the normal processes."

"We've always been told that," says Cindy, "you don't need us very often, but when you need us, you really need us."

"That is right," says Matson, "And that's why we have to make changes, to make tough decisions, about who takes these roles in the control complexes. "

"So how did you know to override two votes this time?" asks Cindy. " It could have been us being removed from the programme."

"Look, on the level with you," says Matson, "It is not just one situation here, there have been at least 10 anomalies from each of the other teams."

"What about us?" I ask.

"Just twice," says Matson, "The first was a long time ago.

"You were the first of the three teams to make an error. Then no errors until one a few weeks ago. Since then, perfect. With the other teams, there has been a progressive increase over the last two months. The last situation was part of a short run of four in the last three weeks. It's enough to create a major problem for us."

"Is that how we came into the roles?" asks Cindy. "When we were appointed, we had been acting as backup for the previous team. The difference is we were told they were being given launch priorities and moving out to Moon Two and probably on to Ganymede itself."

"That's right," says Matson, "The previous team went to Moon Two. The change in schedules of the outbound fleets has meant that they are still candidates for Ganymede."

"It really is up or out," I muse.

"You could say that" says Matson. "You remember that you have some of the most prestigious roles in the complex."

"So, this is what will happen," says Matson, "Firstly, I wanted to tell you about the situation. Then I want to explain about your counterparts in the other complexes. As you know, we deliberately keep you separated and the same will apply with the new replacements. It makes no difference to your relationships with your own backup team, who I'm sure you know well."

"What you will need to know is that your own Prime images will now be used by the other teams as a starting point."

"After that, each team will run its own way and it will only be when there are new voting situations, we must again crosscheck the outcomes."

"And does ours get reset too?" I ask.

"No," says Matson, "But with your rate of error being so low, it will be many years before you would reach 10. And by the way, 10 isn't a magic number here. What we've just experienced is a highly rapid increase in discrepancies from the other teams."

"Now, do you have questions for me? I'd like us all to get back to business as usual as soon as possible."

I look at Cindy. There are many questions, but sense it would be pointless to ask,

Matson pressed a small button on his desk. A tall, attractive woman with blonde pulled back hair and wearing a charcoal grey outfit appeared. I noticed Cindy checking my reaction.

"Hello," she smiled professionally. "You must be Cindy and Sam? Let me escort you back to the main lobby."

We knew we should wait until we were away from the block before discussing what that just happened. We walked back to the transit pod area.

"We should stop somewhere on our way back," I say, "Maybe grab a coffee. It'll give us a chance to chat."

Cindy nods back, knowingly, "Yes, we pretty much used up the morning in any case."

We walk into a nearby mall. There is a food court and a couple of empty tables by a waterfall feature. I hope the sound will mask our conversation.

Cindy asks, "So what do we know from that?"

I pause, realising I'm getting suckered into the dream. It is all feeling so real. Surely this can't last for the next five years?

"Okay," I say, "Let's start with what we know about Earthside. The entire New Delaware facility is run by Torus industries. They have seen through the acceleration of the space program to support Ganymede. Torus has been a consolidation of several other companies, including Biotree and Brant Industry, which had developed much of the advanced technology prevalent on Ganymede and Earthside."

Cindy adds, "There seem to be two other equivalent huge corporations operating in other parts of the world. *AlfaCorporatsiya* (AlfaCorp) for Eurussia and *Kǎxīmǔ gōngyè* (Cassim Gongje) for Sino-Nihon.

"Ganymede has individual areas, each being mined by one of the large industry conglomerates.

"For those that worked at Torus, it was considered a privilege. Since the Klima Wars wiped out large parts of the Earth, there had been fewer high-profile roles within which to operate."

"Whoa, stop there..."I say, "The Klima Wars?"

"Yes, there were two periods of unrest called the Scourge and the Klima Wars during which Earth super-powers fought over access to the remaining earth resources. It started with oil reserves but soon affected everything. Energy, Food supplies, Water."

I realise that RightDream must be backfilling history.

Cindy continued, "The work involved with the space shuttles to Ganymede was still a high-level engineering task suited to scientists, although much of the Earth's work was now geared toward food production.

"The smaller global population meant that there were sustainable foodstuffs left in the remaining habitable parts of Earth however the food tech had also moved to greater synthesis, implying fewer proper foodstuffs to eat in many parts of the world.

"The three global bands of Earthside had seen this occur. Most of the scientists lived in the middle band, which is where New Delaware was situated."

The 'three global bands' were also new information to me.

Cindy continues, "Considerably south of the facility was the start of the desert plains, which led to the uninhabitable desolation areas.

"A similar climactic effect occurred within the sea and it now contains potentially dangerous chemicals and is unsuitable for to use for transport. Wherever water is needed, there are new large-scale desalination units of the type used previously in desert areas to take the saltwater and purify it so that it could be used for supporting life.

"The New Delaware facility, like many other major

population areas, was largely enclosed. Although people would go outdoors in this zone, they would attempt to limit their exposure to sunlight and to the unscrubbed atmosphere."

I assume it is RightDream providing context.

Torus was one of the major conglomerates and also provided the clothing and other climate management facilities on Earth. After the full perils of climate change had become clear, pre-existing industries needed to pool their resources to develop the relevant remedies.

There was still competition, but the scale of the endeavours was such that in each of the major continental zones a single company emerged as the leader to provide the coverage necessary.

 A few people had arisen in each of these companies and acted as sovereign rulers in the relevant areas. Earth Council had established a forum structure to provide regulation and many of the pre-war countries were represented through a kind of Senate.

However, there was a great need for speed to develop the required changes and Torus had used strong leadership to drive through its approach to the space program, to robotics, to climate management and to the feeding and wellbeing of the remaining population.

The economic model had changed. There was still currency and exchange rates between nations, but most people would exist using tokens which were charged at the beginning of a month and which included pre-allocated deductions for food, transport, and other necessary aspects of living.

In return for this, most people living in New Delaware could expect a stable lifestyle in exchange for their contribution through work. It was a very different role from the capitalist approach used prior to the start of the climate decline.

There were few people left who remembered the world before the change to the new regime.

Communications, education, discussions about freedoms were all contained within this limited framework. Astride it all was Torus Corporation and the other similar sized behemoths.

Back in the 21st-century there had still been around 200 countries and 20 major nation states that dictated how politics and major economics operated on Earth.

The shifts in population and wealth and the redistribution of natural resources because of the climactic changes meant that this number now reduced to a smaller number of nation states, with transnational corporations gaining the upper hand.

There had always been corporations joining and splitting themselves to optimise their global footprint to gain the greatest economic and political advantages, whilst often paying the lowest taxation.

The situation with global corporations was not new and had origins right back to the Second World War when companies such as Cola manufacturers would retain both an Amerikan *"It's the real thing"* and a German *"Mach doch mal Pause"* presence. In effect, playing on both sides of the equation.

The three largest corporations together ran via

subsidiaries and covered approximately 70% of the Earth's major businesses.

The major stakeholders in the corporations were now nation-states who contributed towards the shareholding of the companies and in return received the income streams necessary to sustain their populations.

The decline in the habitability of the southern hemisphere also meant that the three corporations operated from above the equator. Closest to the Equator were the reception areas for the return of the miners from Ganymede. The base in the Americas was the one in New Delaware and there were equivalent control locations in Europe's Barcelona and China's Shenhua.

"So, what will we do next?" asks Cindy.

Swapping Primes

"Let's think," says Cindy, "Matson decided the futures for the two Prime teams he needed to stand down."

I ask, "Do you believe him when he says they have been peacefully redistributed, you know, to other duties?"

"Maybe, but how ever we look at it, it's a demotion. And come to think of it, we heard nothing else from the people we replaced."

"You think they might have been terminated?"

"In Brant's world, there are other options. They could also have met with a 'water-ski' accident. Remember, the fully functioning bodies of humans are a tradable asset nowadays."

Cindy looks at me. I can see she is wracking her brain to look for any other signs of what is happening. I also sense that there are self-imposed guard rails on what we may think about. It is RightDream not letting us spin off into wild supposition.

Keeping us on track.

I suggest, "Matson must also know that his Primes are a valuable and scarce resource. It must put pressure on him?"

Cindy nods, "He knows his teams of Primes were valuable, but that they could not be left where they could discover and highlight anomalies. It throws his whole programme into question."

"But what about trading out his Primes for those of, say, Sino-Nihon or Eurussia?"

"It would be a negotiation, because the Sino-Nihon and Eurussians would both probably want to swap with Amerika - you know, to find out things - like industrial espionage?"

"And there's a rumour that the Eurussians have taken the unprecedented step of removing all three of their teams based upon a similar incident to ours."

"All three? They must have discovered something. Something big."

"Yes, and that's why Matson is so keen to cover everything up now."

Torus Industries

The Sunshine Mall Food court we had selected included a dumbed-down streamcom service targeting passing foot-traffic. The whole complex was run by Torus Industries.

Torus was established approximately 50 years earlier and had seen through the acceleration of the space program to support Ganymede. There had been a consolidation of several other companies, including Biotree and Brant, which developed much of the nanotechnology prevalent on Ganymede and Earthside. Torus was a peaceful corporation symbolised with the logo of a curvaceous lotus mandala. It was an ideal way to hide the military contractor capabilities of Brant Industries behind peaceful branding.

AlfaCorporatsiya (AlfaCorp) for Eurussia and *Kăxīmŭ gōngyè* (Cassim Gongje) for Sino-Nihon had both achieved similar disguises, most famous for the clean-up after the Ukrainian War, where both AlfaCorp and Cassim Gongje had been involved in lucrative reconstruction. Ironic, considering that AlfaCorp had supplied many of the weapons for the first Klima War.

Working directly for Torus was considered a privilege. Since the Scourge and then the Klima War had wiped out large parts of the planet Earth, there had been a few higher profile roles within which to operate. Most of these were in the Headquarters operations of Torus, AlfaCorp and Cassim Gongje. The work involved with the space shuttles to Ganymede was still a high-level engineering task.

The wider Earthside roles were now geared toward food production. The smaller global population meant there were sustainable foodstuffs left in the remaining habitable parts of Earth. Food tech had moved to greater synthesis which implied fewer organic foodstuffs to eat in many parts of the world.

Considerably south of the facilities was the start of desert plains which led in turn to the desolation areas that were considered uninhabitable.

Torus also provided the clothing and other climate management facilities on earth. After the full perils of climate change had become clear, the pre-existing industries needed to pool their resources to develop the relevant remedies quickly.

There was still competition, but the scale of the endeavours was such that in each of the major continental zones a single company emerged to provide the coverage necessary.

 A few leaders had arisen in each of these companies and acted as sovereign rulers of the relevant areas. Earth Council had established a forum structure to provide regulation and many of the pre-war countries were represented through a kind of Senate.

However, there was a great need for speed to develop the required changes and Torus driven through its approach to the space program, to robotics, to climate management and to the feeding and wellbeing of the remaining population.

The economic model had changed. There was still

currency and exchange rates between nations, but most people existed using tokens which were charged at the beginning of a month and which included pre-allocated deductions for food, transport, and other necessary aspects of living. It was the so-called 'table-stakes' of being an Earthside dweller.

Communications, education, discussions about freedoms were all contained within this limited framework. Astride it all was Torus Corporation and the other similar sized behemoths. Back in the 21st-century there were 200 countries and 20 major nation states that dictated how politics and major economics operated on earth. Now, shifts in population, wealth, and the redistribution of natural resources because of the climactic changes meant transnational corporations gained the upper hand.

The situation with global corporations was not new and had origins right back to the Second World War when companies such as Cola manufacturers would retain both an Amerikan *"It's the real thing"* and a German *"Mach doch mal Pause"* presence. In effect, playing on both sides of the equation.

The three largest corporations together ran via subsidiaries and covered approximately 70% of the Earth's major businesses.

The major stakeholders in the corporations were now nation-states who contributed towards the shareholding of the companies and in return received the income streams necessary to sustain their populations.

The decline in the habitability of the southern hemisphere also meant that the three corporations operated from above the equator. Closest to the Equator were the reception areas for the return of the miners from Ganymede. The base in the Americas was the one in New Delaware, and there were equivalent control locations in Europe's Barcelona and China's Shenhua.

Nozzles

Cindy gestures toward the Streamcom in the Mall.

"That didn't take very long!" she whispers. "Look - we're famous!"

A story was playing about how we were both caught up in a security break-in at The Block. It said nothing bad about us, but implied that we had been abducted and were probably being hidden somewhere. The photos looked as if they had been taken from our recent visit to The Block. New Secondaries had been brought into the control room to substitute for us both.

There was a short cut-away to Matson, in the control room with the two Secondaries - neither of whom I recognised but identified by their different uniform flashes. They were both quietly operating the controls. A streamcom interviewer was asking the Secondaries what they knew about the situation.

"We have been on duty since yesterday, ", says one of the Secondaries. It looks as if they were using the Secondaries to cover up our last time on duty.

"And have you noticed anything unusual during your time in operation?" asked the interviewer. I looked at the background display and could see Cindy doing the same. The base was showing an Amber base alert, but no other untoward status lights displayed.

"Amber base alert," says Cindy, "It must be just for us!"

The first Secondary continued talking, "There's nothing especially unusual from the last period. Except, when we were first brought online, there was a short-term irregularity. An incoming ship had to be steered around a meteorite shower, and the course correction was re-applied late because of a security anomaly."

"At the same time that it was occurring, a large download of archival data was requested," continued the Secondary. "The strange thing is, I can't see the archive repository folder for the download. It's fairly unusual, as if the download has disappeared."

"That's it," says Cindy, "We are being framed for a data theft."

We both jump from our seats. This is just what is needed to get us both rounded up, but with only a vague hint of any wrongdoing.

"They will deploy Hunters, I expect," says Cindy.

She was referring to the special police force whose sole role was to hunt for people who were sought for further enquiries.

"We've still got some time," I say.

"Time to get some distance," answers Cindy.

"We'll have to move into The Scratch," says Cindy.

I don't think I even knew about The Scratch before I was placed into this RightDream. Now I seemed to have expert knowledge. The Scratch is an unregulated area with an estimated population of 20 million. Each of the main routes into the area had warning signs discouraging people from entering. The zone still uses older technologies and has created a sustainable ecosystem using materials that are now banned from most of the rest of the planet and certainly from the rest of Amerika.

The area and a few others like it around the world were set up as part of a series of deals when the modern technology arrived to replace the crumbled legacy from the systems that were dying. Not everyone was prepared to step into the new ways of working, which requires everyone to buy into support for what would become the new ecosystem with its far more regulated ways of living, in return for a higher quality of perceived lifestyle.

The new approach supposedly provides a better level of consumerist lifestyle in return for curtailment of certain previous civil liberties.

Most people were content to live in what was a type of totalitarian state. The governing processes meant everyone must work, and in return, the leisure time was improved, although the range of preferred leisure pursuits was also restricted.

But in the Scratch, life was different. It was here the people who had dropped out of the squeaky-clean society lived. It was a messy tangle of bazaars, strip-mall based shopping and scrappy road networks. The power sources were still often organic-based, and this created a haze across much of the zone. Some older tech was available for power provision, but it was mainly provided by units that were now considered defunct in the rest of the main capital cities.

The location of Scratch was a consequence of the location of major population centres on the eastern seaboard of the old USA. Set between major population centres of New York, Boston, and Washington D.C. and close to the New Delaware space complex, it had become the automatic choice for outsiders to live and create a living.

Some said the area had once been called New Jersey, although the area directly south of Manhattan had acquired the Jersey name and the records of a New Jersey were patchy.

There had been various gang wars in the mid-21st century around this part of the world, although not much was known about the detail.

In my false memory generated by RightDream, I had visited the Scratch like so many other well-heeled tourists, but I am seeing it now through very different eyes.

We reach a road. A traditional tarmac strip, wide enough for passing traffic, although seemingly lightly used at present. In the distance, we can see the higher buildings of the Scratch, in its most populous part. In the opposite direction, we could see the sparkle from the tall and glittering buildings of New Delaware.

"We'll need to get someone to take us to downtown Scratch," I say. "Let's get over to that road. We may get someone to take us using Landtran."

The road system inside the Scratch differed from anything that we were used to. The main transit units were carbon powered. They were mainly running on biofuels, which were being manufactured somewhere within the Scratch. Most transport was small and lightweight. Adapted and powered bicycles, tiny cars, and an occasional larger transport unit for carrying goods or large quantities of people.

As we approached the road, we could see one of the large people carriers. We hailed it and it stopped. Our uniforms identified us as people from outside of the Scratch, although most people would recognise us and realise that we would have access to money from New Delaware.

The driver looks towards us. He asks to see our money. We show him our money from New Delaware.

"I will need to take it all," says the driver. "I will give you back each enough for two day's food. The rest is now the property of the Scratch." We knew better than to argue and climbed onto the bus.

"Here," said the driver, "This token is valid for the whole day. You can travel anywhere."

We settle back into the seats on the bus. Those around us look with tired interest at these two strangers from New Delaware. Cindy clutches at her bag. I can see she is concerned that the other passengers may decide to rob her. The two of us could not fend off a full busload of people if they got angry.

"You will be safe while you ride this bus," says the driver.

"They can see you have paid a considerable sum, which will enter the Scratch economy."

He turned to the passengers. "They also note that I have protection devices on this bus, so if there is any trouble I will deploy," He spoke with a mask above his head and now lowered it back onto his face.

We look up above the seats to see small nozzles projecting into each of the seating areas. Not for ventilation, they were to release some kind of toxin if there was trouble on the bus. The driver could don protection, but we did not want to have to experience the effects of a bus fight.

"How long will it take us to get to the centre?" I ask.

"We are already close," says the driver, "Another 10 minutes and we should be as close as I can take you on this bus."

There was a pre-recorded announcement on the public address system of the bus.

"This will be a selected disembarkation point only. Nominated passengers may alight."

We notice all the other passengers are wearing electronically secured seat belts. We wonder why the driver had not done this for us.

The driver looks back towards Cindy, "I know why you are here," he says, "You certainly picked an unusual way to arrive."

He slowed the bus and indicated to the front right, "You

are about one minute from the central area," he says. "Just go along that pathway and you will be there within a minute. Look for the trikes."

We disembarked from the bus. There are acrid smells in the air. We are both used to the scrubbed air of New Delaware. This was a completely different sensation.

"That's the smell of cooking," says Cindy, "They have organics here and are cooking with them."

 We cross into the square and look around for signs of anyone that might be looking for them. Cindy notices that there were several groups of people standing at the exits from the square.

"Something is wrong," she says. "This could be a trap."

 At that moment, a green flash arcs across the square. It was a ribbon wave.

"Look out!" I shout. "I think they are trying to cut us off."

Another ribbon wave flashes across another part of the square. They both appear to be aimed at a tall, blonde man and two companions, both of whom are wearing New Delaware uniforms.

 "We had better turnaround," says Cindy. At that moment, a third flash. The three ribbon waves had now created a triangle with the man and the two uniforms in one corner. The ribbon lines start to contract.

 "They have those people trapped," says Cindy. "We must get away from here."

We move slowly towards a different corner of the square.

We intermingle with the trikes. Someone rings a bell.

"Need a ride?" a man's voice asks. "It'll cost you a day's food in credits."

We look toward the person asking them a question. A taxi driver using one of the trikes. We climb on.

"I've been asked to do this," says the driver, "By that man who has just been cornered by the ribbon waves. I'm getting you moved away and to somewhere safe. I just hope you have the data to make the trade worth it."

He pushes the trike into a road and slowly pedals away from the still visible ribbon wave, which has captured several people. They could see someone moving toward the captured people. It moved like an early android.

"Where are we going?" asks Cindy.

"Somewhere safe," says the driver. He was listening to a police channel on his taxi-com.

The system clicked. A small message. "Hunter has traced Sven. Brought him in."

"What about the Primes? Sam and Cindy," a voice asks. To us, it sounds like Matson.

"No, we just have Sven at present. He was apprehended with two others wearing New Delaware uniforms. We have identified the two in uniforms as residents of The Scratch - in other words, decoys."

"Who is Sven?" asked Cindy, "And who are you?"

The trike driver is moving expertly through the chaotic environment of the Scratch. It has only been two or three minutes since we were picked up.

"Look," says the driver, "You will know about Sven soon enough. He's just been trapped in those ribbon waves with two decoys for each of you. A brave man. Right now, you need to trust me. We need to get away from this area quickly. In a moment, we will be switching to a bullet train."

I knew about bullet trains from the history archives. They had been used for fast transport of many people, but were limited in where they could go, because of the need to run on rails.

The trike driver approaches a staging area from the road surface to the train and asks us to disembark. All three of us climb aboard the train for an immediate departure.

Once inside the train, there was a soft acceleration as it starts to slip away from the station, picking up speed quickly.

"I didn't know Scratch transport was so good," I say to the taxi driver.

"It's making me feel queasy," says Cindy. "I think it is looking at those passing electric gantries."

A few moments later there is a flash like a bolt of lightning, and after a few seconds, a loud explosion. No debris, though.

The trike driver shouts, "They must have ordered a 'destroy' instruction. That will have wiped out a large section of the Scratch."

Cindy asks, "Was that because of us?"

"Yes," answers the trike driver, "You had better have something worthwhile to show us to compensate for all of that damage."

The bullet train was slowing to stop at another conurbation within the Scratch.

The trike driver stood to alight. He smiles and gestures for us to disembark. "My name's Haruto, I'm a colleague of Sven."

Cindy looks at me.

"Sven?" she asks.

Haruto smiles. "Sven, the person who engineered your rescue. I guess he hides in the shadows. He seems to have nine lives."

We are out of the bullet train now and Haruto guides us towards a large grey structure. It looks as if it would have been a shopping warehouse, but now it seems to have fallen into disuse.

He leads us inside, and we are greeted by vintage technology. An X-Blade ship, a couple of 'bots and a bank of flatscreen monitors. I can see cables snaking up the wall and realise we are in some kind of communication centre.

Haruto leads us into another rundown warehouse. In it there is a complete capsule from a space fleet ship. Next to it stands a freighter module.

The ship and freighter module don't look like a standard type.

"It's old," says Haruto, "Third-Generation; I know things have moved on, but there still an awful lot of good technology inside."

"Where did you get this?" I ask.

"It's one prototype from New Delaware, factory fresh," answers Haruto, "It was made by Torus industry as part of the development effort. In those days the Scratch was still used as a feeder zone for New Delaware. Then, from around the time I was removed from duties, they stopped using the Scratch for any kind of work with the space program. They decided it would be more cost efficient to build the ships in space, from Moon Two."

Haruto continues, "It's around the same time that the new fourth-generation ships appeared from Ganymede. They must have started another development site somewhere else to create the streamlining of the fourth generation and beyond."

Fourth Generation…We are well into the future. I guess our original Elysium fleet was First Generation. It's confirmation that I'm in a RightDream based sometime in the future.

Cindy speaks, "Your ship here looks completely different from the later ones. I can see there is a much larger human habitation zone on here."

"The piece we need is the processor deck, even better if it's got a science officer option," I say. "Can we boot up the command deck?"

"Sure," says Haruto, "But if we fire up these systems, we need to be sure they won't attempt to communicate with New Delaware again. We have kept this thing concealed here for many years. We don't want to suddenly break cover in a way that means we will have it taken away from us."

Cindy and I look over the ship. I can't explain where our expertise comes from, except to think it is still a convincing RightDream.

"I can see that there will be some problems if we don't spend some time on this first," I say. Cindy nods her agreement.

"Two things: One, we will need to build a shield around the outside of the ship and second, we will need to ensure that the entire Communications Deck is disabled. Then we should be able to fire up the Command Deck and use the processors."

Cindy agrees. "This really needs more than two people to get everything done. It may seem a little crazy, but we need to get this whole ship running but with no connection to the external world."

Haruto smiles, "You've come to the right place then," he says, "I should explain I am more than a trike driver. I was Sven's colleague when we were Primes back in generation three. The whole of my crew is here. My leading engineer is Tatsuya. We also have the both the Secondaries and the backup teams. Thanks to Sven, we were the last generation of operators to get out of New Delaware after we were decommissioned.

"So how many of you are there?" asks Cindy.

"There were twelve of us," answered Haruto. "Eleven now that Sven has gone."

"There's only nine in a crew nowadays," I say, "And they are talking about reducing it further."

I know there's fifteen in our Agnus Dei crew, but the words just won't come out.

"Our crew had more manual tasks to perform," answers Haruto, "And we know our way around the ships too."

"Yes, that's a difference," says Cindy, "by the time the fifth-generation were in use, we were not allowed to touch the actual ships any longer. They have far more autonomous controls within them now. Nearly the entire return trip is run automatically."

Haruto nods. "That's what we were expecting, " he says.

"Can we switch on the lights, at least?" asks Cindy.

"Yes," says Haruto, "We've already isolated the safety systems and removed the beaconing. It means we can at least see our way around on the ship while we figure out how to disable the rest of the systems."

"We will also need to build some kind of jammer system," I reply, "To ensure that the outer walls of this shed are not leaking any information which could be picked up by new Delaware control."

"We're going to need a lot of cable for that. I really want to make this shed disappear from radio detection completely."

Cindy asks, "What about a chicken fence? Make a

Faraday cage around the ship?"

"We have plenty of chicken fencing here in the Scratch," says Haruto, "And chickens, come to that. But now, come with me. There is something else I can show you."

He moved towards a small shed within the facility. He opened the door and showed a stack of white containers.

"These are magnetite motors," he announces. "We have kept them secret and they have never been started."

"These are great. They can be used to both fire up the control deck and also be used to help create the jammer field around the shed."

"They are all addressable, though," cautions Cindy, "If we start them, they will send out control signals."

"Give me a toolbox," I say, surprising myself at this new knowledge.

Tatsuya appears. "Hi," he says, "Sorry to get straight to business, but you two are both sending out signals from your ident chips. I have probably disabled around 60 of these chips. In the early days, we used to remove them. It was very messy. Once we had a few to examine, we worked out that their pairing uses the body as a personal area network. The trick is to disable both parts at exactly the same moment.

"And how do you do this?" asked Sam.

"Nowadays we use a high voltage shock to blow out both chips simultaneously. If we only do one of them, it will fire the tamper protocols in the other chip. It sends a blocking signal to the central nervous system. Not pretty.

"If we fire the voltage at the same moment to both chips, they fry, and you will be okay. The downside is if you have any uploads built inside of you. You know; extra skill sets like languages, machine analytics.

"Also, I don't think you will be able to have any further adaptations after this," says Tatsuya.

"But it will remove the identities from us? Make us go invisible to searches?" asked Cindy.

"That's right," says Tatsuya, "I should warn you that the high-voltage is applied like an ECT shock. You will be disabled for an hour or more after we have done it."

"Would you prefer to both be done at the same time or to wait until one of you is recovered before the other one goes through this?" asks Tatsuya.

Haruto replies, "At this point, it would be better if you were both put through the procedure together. There's a simple reason for this. It will minimise the remaining time that they can access your identity sensors."

"What is the procedure?" asked Cindy, " When I've seen this in a movie, it all looks pretty horrific."

"I still need the high voltage that they use routinely for this, but I can apply unilaterally to just one side of your head and before I administer, I can give you both an anaesthetic and a muscle relaxant. This will make the whole thing recoverable more quickly.

"Okay," I say, " but tell me how many times you have done this?"

"For 60 Idents we have de-chipped I have probably used this on 40."

"And what is your strike rate?" I ask.

"Thirty-seven," answers Tatsuya. "We had three failures."

"And what happened to them?" asks Cindy.

"Each one had abnormalities in their chipset. They had been changed but in ways we could not detect until we administered the ECT."

I look at Cindy, "I don't think we have any choice in this."

Cindy nods.

"Okay, where do we need to go for this?" she asks.

"It'll blow your mind, " says Tatsuya, indicating a back room, "Follow me."

अचिन्त्यभेदाभेद

Achintya-Bheda-Abheda (अचिन्त्यभेदाभेद) is a school of Vedanta representing the philosophy of inconceivable one-ness and difference.

In Sanskrit achintya means 'inconceivable', bheda translates as 'difference', and abheda translates as 'non-difference.'

The Gaudiya Vaishnava religious tradition employs the term in relation to the relationship of creation and creator (Krishna, Svayam Bhagavan) between God and his energies.

It is believed that this philosophy was taught by the movement's theological founder in the late 15th Century, Chaitanya Mahaprabhu and differentiates the Gaudiya tradition from the other Vaishnava Sampradayas.

It can be understood as an integration of the strict dualist (dvaita) theology of Madhvacharya and the qualified monism (vishishtadvaita) of Ramanuja.

Vaishnavism

Within Puranic literatures and general Vaiśnava philosophy *tattva* is often used to denote certain categories or types of being or energies such as:

Viṣṇu-tattva: The Supreme God. The causative factor of everything including other Tattvas

Kṛṣṇa-tattva: Any incarnation or expansion of Śrī Narayan/Krishna.

Śakti-Tattva: The multifarious energies of Śrī Kṛṣṇa. It includes his internal potency, Yoga Maya, and material prakṛti.

Jīva-tattva: The living souls or jivas.

Śiva-tattva: Śrī Śiva (excluding Rudras) is not considered to be a jiva.

Mahat-tattva: The total material energy (*prakṛti*).

Govinda Jaya Jaya

I notice Haruto and Tatsuya's slick professionalism as they prep us for the removal of the ident trackers. They are going to process us both together, but I sense that I'll still be the first. I'm placed upon an operating table and wired up in a way that reminds me of the RightMind process. Except this time, I'm being zapped with a high voltage close to my brain to blow out some difficult internal circuits.

Tatsuya recites a small chant to both of us, and I notice in Cindy's case it works like a switch has been flipped and she becomes ultra-docile. I can't tell whether anything similar has worked for me.

Govinda Jaya Jaya
Gopala Jaya Jaya
Radha-ramanahari
Govinda Jaya Jaya

Then, I'm suddenly in a bright nightclub. I hear Tattva being repeated.

Achintya-Bheda-Abheda, Tattva
Achintya-Bheda-Abheda, Tattva"

I have to remind myself that I'm still under the spell of RightDream. I'm not really in this Hangar. Not really with these people. This is supposed to be helping me get to Ganymede.

I hear music and Cindy approaches me. A band is singing.

Like the flower and the scent of summer
Like the sun and the shine,
Well, the truth may come in strange disguises
Send a message to your mind

At the moment that you wake from sleeping
And you know it's all a dream
Well, the truth may come in strange disguises
Never knowing what it means

For you shall be tomorrow
Like you have been today
If this was never ending
What more can you say?

Achintya-Bheda-Abheda, Tattva
Achintya-Bheda-Abheda, Tattva

But I remember I'm still alone. Alone on the Agnus Dei. This reconstruction is from RightDream, and it seems to know about the future.

PART THREE - AWAKEN

Chandelier

One, two, three, one, two, three, drink
One, two, three, one, two, three, drink
One, two, three, one, two, three, drink
Throw 'em back 'til I lose count

I'm gonna swing from the chandelier
From the chandelier
I'm gonna live like tomorrow doesn't exist
Like it doesn't exist
I'm gonna fly like a bird through the night
Feel my tears as they dry
I'm gonna swing from the chandelier
From the chandelier
But I'm holding on for dear life

Won't look down, won't open my eyes
Keep my glass full until morning light
'Cause I'm just holding on for tonight
Help me, I'm holding on for dear life
Won't look down, won't open my eyes
Keep my glass full until morning light
'Cause I'm just holding on for tonight
On for tonight

Sia Kate Furler and Jesse Shatkin

Waking in sweats

There's a sudden jolt and I'm awake again. I've been thrown out of the imaginary hangar. I awaken and feel the blood pulsing through my head and hear my heartbeat in my left ear. The music has changed to massive bounce Terranation beats at around 160 bpm.

I'm sweating as I realise I've been boosted by the wake-up drug from the LifePod. Like a bump of molly, it makes me feel hyper-alert. It is a big hit because it takes me another minute to decode the sounds around me. The warble that I'd first heard when I was climbing into the pod. A rising tone, first long and then a shorter one. Its big news from the bad dream hotline.

Next, I hit the big buttons on the remote to remove myself from the LifePod and as climb out I can see the other pods are RedLit.

Red light on a pod means no life. The small screens on each pod present further readouts. I wonder how much amphetamine I am struggling through, because each of the pods shows signs of life on their small readouts.

Maybe I'm hallucinating from the amphetamines? I

decide to jack one of the other pods to see what is happening.

A nearby Viewer lets me break into the neural flow of the LifePod and its occupant. I'd have to route the Viewer to a single LifePod and rig myself up with a RightMind so that I could see what was happening to the occupant.

But first, I need to shut down the noise. At least gravity is normal, so I find a repeater console for the main deck. Here I can see the alerts displayed. More red than green. I run my finger along the column marked reset, and most of the reds change to blue (meaning acknowledged) and mercifully the alert sounds switch off.

I think that BlueLit isn't much better than red, but at least I can hear myself think. I can also feel a deadening of my own responses as the speed drug works its way out of my system. I see no point in contacting Mission Control. They are several minutes behind me.

I grab a RightMind helmet and plug it into a Viewer next to the LifePods. As I look at the Viewer, I realise we are only on Mission Day 200. Less than a year into the mission. We have only travelled less that a sixth of the way to Jupiter. Maybe Mission Control is more accessible that I thought?

I look for a RightComm socket on the outside of another LifePod. I hook up the connections and place the RightMind on my head.

RightMind

I feel the RightMind take control. I've picked LifePod 3
James K. Andersen: Flight Engineer I.

James and I are both well versed in the ways of the ship.
He's running an R.E.M track with a background scene
from something that looks like Caravaggio:

I thought that I heard you laughing
I thought that I heard you sing
I think I thought I saw you try
But that was just a dream
Try, cry, fly, try
That was just a dream
Just a dream

Andersen seems completely locked into the music.
Maybe the LifePod induced sleep is working better for
him than it did for me, although I still can't work out why
his pod is showing a Red status.

Maybe I should try a different LifePod? I select Charlotte
Ridley in LifePod 2. She is the Mission Specialist and
seems to be running silently. No music, no special effects.
I consider that this should make her easier to tap into.

Charlotte Ridley seems alert - almost as if she is on the same drug that I was when I awoke. She seems to have a natural talent for RightMind communication. She notices me immediately and is trying to tell me something. It's about someone else. Someone called Lekton. I've never heard of him but write the name down so that I won't forget.

I'm struggling to remember that this is the real world again and not the RightDream.

Charlotte explains she has been approached by Lekton, to change part of the Agnus Dei mission. I don't understand. Charlotte explains Lekton has found a way to communicate to her through her RightMind and wants to cut a deal. It still doesn't make much sense to me.

I don't know who Lekton is, nor why or how he would be out here in space.

"Lekton said he wants to be elected to the Earth Council. To be one of the Senate. He wants the Amerika Earth Controller seat on the Trinity. That if he wins it, he will be able to control Ganymede 'droids remotely from Earthside. To do that, he asked if I would help him get back to Earth. In return, he will re-instate my LifePod and another one which can carry him."

This was all getting very weird. I'd always thought of Charlotte as a down-to-earth individual with a clear head. None of this made sense.

"But what has happened to our crew?" I ask.

"Don't you see?" asks Charlotte. "We were all switched.

Lekton inhabited the ship and then ran a remote shutdown. You escaped because your LifePod was set to Manual Override. The rest of us have been switched."

"Switched?" I query.

"Yes, switched to the secondary systems. The ones in the XTend BrainCore."

I suddenly realise that I am talking to a sheep brain facsimile of Charlotte. And that the rest of the crew are also trapped in the XTend titanium box.

"They didn't explain that if you get switched, it is a one-way trip," says Charlotte.

"I don't seem to be able to talk to the rest of the crew," I say, "Just to you."

"No, you must use the direct link to the XTend, not relay in via the LifePod."

"How is it that yours works?" I ask.

"I don't know. Lekton explained he has boosted my individual capabilities. I am wary of him, though. I suspect it is some form of trap."

As she spoke, I could feel something very light passing across my head. It was as if a spider or small insect had become trapped in my hair. I assumed it was Lekton having a look around.

"I'm going to bail!" I shiver as I say it.

"Probably the right thing to do," answers Charlotte.

I lift the RightMind from my head and am immediately placed back into the daunting environment of a spacecraft with no crew heading fast from Earth to the still distant Jupiter.

Turn around

An advantage of being a Flight Engineer is that I get to know how most of the systems on the spacecraft work.

By comparison, the miners would only have rudimentary electro-mechanical knowledge and, aside from James, Flight Engineer 1, only the pilot would have similar knowledge to me, but far less practical than mine. After all, I get to operate the ship's controls and deal with problems and workarounds.

It's strange. Often, we don't register the important moments in our lives as they happen. We only see that they were important when we look back.

Like, that was an ending. So was that.

And that was...That was the beginning of something. Something massive.

Maybe something massive and awful. Really awful. Like, mess-up-your-whole-life awful.

Right now, I have two immediate priorities:

1) Inform Earth of the prevailing conditions
2) Figure out how to get back, either directly or via a rescue operation.

I use one of the repeater consoles to check possibilities. We are moving through space so fast, it will take a miracle to figure out how to turn around.

Fortunately, our SpaceNav comes up with some options:

1) Reverse thrust the engines, stop, rotate, and restart. Success probability: 27% - Possible outcomes: a) loss of fuel b) stopping distance is another year of flight c) damage to engines during braking manoeuvre d) complexity of rotation manoeuvre and stress to sides of the ship. e) Insufficient fuel left to restart for return trip.

In other words, it is like turning a 20th Century seafaring super tanker.

2) Continue. Success probability: 34% - Possible outcomes: a) loss of life support because of keeping one human alive b) health damage [Mental and Physical] because of five years in space.

3) Slingshot return to Earth. Success probability: 88% - Possible Outcomes: a) misalignment b) timing the slingshot to a direct space object. c) reliance on autopilot and RightMind navigation. d) complexity of turn manoeuvre and stress to the ship

I scan the options. I notice there is no rescue option. The only one which looks viable is option 3. It requires us to locate an object which we can use to slingshot around, thereby preserving our speed but executing a 'U' turn in space.

I ask SpaceNav to develop Option 3. It finds a brilliant sub-option. The dwarf planet Ceres is on an oddly shaped orbit which runs between Mars and Jupiter. SpaceNav identifies a point of rendezvous in around two months, when we are close enough to be catapulted back towards earth whilst maintaining our already gained speed.

I consider running it past Mission Control, but instead lock it in on the console. I ask for an estimate of how long to reach Earth again. It responds with 187 days. That's around 6 months with me awake and consuming supplies. I realise that the supplies for the last 36 days in the original mission should give enough of everything for me to survive the return trip. 15 people times 36 days = 540 person days of supplies is about triple the amount that I will need.

And an 88% probability of success.

Ceres

Ceres is an interesting chunk of rock. It hangs out in the asteroid belt between Mars and Jupiter, and with its 952-kilometre (592-mile) diameter, it's considered both the largest known asteroid in the Solar System, and the only dwarf planet closer to the Sun than Neptune.

It has been considered for habitation in the past and as an intermediate point for interstellar travel.

So why consider Ceres as a staging post? The motivation is to have a settlement with a gravity that allows growth beyond Earth's living area, while also providing easy intra-settlement travel for the inhabitants and reasonably low population density of 500 people per square kilometre.

Mars and the Moon might not be the best places for human colonies, because their natural gravity is so different from Earth's. We know astronauts face health problems when returning to Earth from a low or Zero-G environment; we have very little idea of the effects of growing to maturity in low gravity.

Fortunately, all the studies of Ceres mean that its vital

statistics are well-known and could be recalled from the SpaceNav.

Then the SpaceNav can calculate an ideal path to pick up orbital energy from Ceres and allow the slingshot of our craft back toward Earth.

But right now, I need to contact Earth to appraise them of current status.

This flight tonight

Look out to the left, the Captain said
The lights down there, that's where we'll land
I saw a falling star burn up
Above the Las Vegas sands
It wasn't the one that you gave to me
That night down south between the trailers

Not the early one
That you can wish upon,
Not the northern one
That guides in the sailors

Blackness everywhere and little lights shine
Oh, blackness, blackness dragging me down
Turn this crazy bird around
Oh, star light, star bright
You've got the lovin' that I like, all right
I shouldn't have got on this flight tonight

Joni Mitchell

Link to Earth

"Mission Control, This is Sam Walker, from Agnus Dei. How do you hear me?"

"We hear you loud and clear, although we were not expecting to hear your direct voice for another four years? You are sending us the monthly recordings, in any case."

I remember that there is an automatic signal sent every 28 days to let Mission Control know that everything is on track.

"Mission Control, we have a problem."

"Repeat, please. It sounded like you have a problem?"

"A Problem. Our LifePods have switched to the XTend system, for all crew members except me, Sam Walker. I am now alone as a single survivor on this flight."

"Copy that, although our repeater monitors don't show the status you are reporting. We have fifteen, I repeat fifteen crew alive and functioning. They are all in cryosleep inside LifePods at present. On course for

Ganymede."

I answer, "Think about it. I'm one of the fifteen, but I'm here out of cryo and talking to you right now. Check LifePod 5 - That's mine."

"Copy that. We are running checks now. We are sending you an identify code. Please recite it back."

I waited. They did not believe mine was a genuine transmission. Then the code arrives and it is a snippet from a poem:

"And blood-black nothingness began to spin
A system of cells interlinked within
Cells interlinked within cells interlinked
Within one stem. And dreadfully distinct
Against the dark, a tall white fountain played"

As I recite it back, I realise it is from that Nabokov book that Lucy gave me - Pale Fire. I momentarily wonder if I'm even talking to the real Mission Control, but then think no-one else would play such a warped trick.

Okay, Sam, calm down, be professional.

Breathe.

Nabokov was playing with his readers, telling his story through the footnotes to a poem. It is like a signal to me.

"Sam, It's Cindy. Explain yourself for Mission Control." I instantly recognise Cindy's voice, but then remember she is an android.

"Where are you? How did you know to be in contact so quickly?"

"I'm Earthside. They contacted me when they received your transmission. They have patched me through to you. I selected the identify code. I'm to help you get back to Moon Two."

'Moon Two,' she's just said, not Earth. I remember about footnotes and off-page references.

Turn this crazy bird around.

"I'm going to turn-around. I won't reach Jupiter in any case."

Cindy replies, "How can you do that?"

"I've used the SpaceNav to predict options and select one. I'm going to slingshot off Ceres, in about 60 days."

"Do you intend to stay awake now?"

"Yes, I can't rely on the LifePods. I think is only because I was on manual controls that my own LifePod didn't switch me in the same way as the others."

"But Mission here is saying you have 15 crew still functioning."

"Trust me, they are all gone. They have been restarted in the BrainCore. I spoke to Charlotte Ridley. She told me she had been approached by an entity called Lekton. That Lekton was trying to cut a deal with her. I'm pretty sure that Lekton somehow took over the control systems on this ship. He quiesced the LifePods and they Switched."

"How will you handle the ship alone?"

"Remember, I'm a Flight Engineer. If I punch in the co-ordinates for the slingshot and then afterwards manually adjust the vectors to bring us back to Moon Two, I can fly the very last part of the routing from the Mission deck."

I suddenly remember, "What about the other flights? Elysium 1-4 and 6-10?"

"The first three arrived on Ganymede. Elysium 4 is due in a matter of days. They are setting up the base right now. And not only the Amerikan Base, but also Sino-Nihon and Eurussia have created Programmes like Elysium. It has turned into another space race. I've already sent you a package"

I knew by package she meant a Newscast, which I could watch on the Agnus Dei's screencast system.

A few seconds later, I am watching a promotional video for the new bases on Ganymede. I realise that the other ships in our fleet were considerably larger than Agnus Dei, to carry both additional people, equipment and building material. They are already harvesting the moon surface of Ganymede for further construction material. With nothing to destroy except a barren, low-gravity moon, the progress on the new mining camp is fast.

A new voice cuts in, "Hi Flight Engineer Sam Walker. This is Commander Don Giessen, Elysium Central Command. It is good to hear from you and we send condolences that there has been an incident on board. We can see that you are planning a manoeuvre to redirect the spacecraft. We cannot agree with your planned manoeuvre, which will stress the space frame of your ship. We recommend you continue the mission and return to your LifePod."

I look around. There's 14 LifePods with lights on but nobody home. Every one of the crew has been swapped out to the XTend system. Surrogate organic sheep brains augmented with highly clocked digital artificial intelligence. I wonder if the crew are experiencing something like that picture by Munch. A single scream, frozen in time from 1893.

I've already decided I'll ride the rest of the way fully conscious.

Newton's Third Law

I was marvelling at Newton's Third Law. He derived it in 1687 and we are still using it to steer spacecraft.

The SpaceNav could do all the heavy calculus to create a gravitational slingshot by the use of the relative movement and gravity of another astronomical object to alter the path and speed of Agnus Dei.

We'd flip around and be heading back toward Earth, or at least toward Moon Two. I could understand the point of Moon Two, with its several mammoth space craft being built there. If they were on earth, it would be like trying to launch Manhattan's Empire State building into space. Instead, we had a collection of micro-moves. Like moving from one apartment to another in a busy metropolis when the main unit of transfer is a taxicab.

I was using the dwarf planet Ceres as my target to bend the Agnus Dei's trajectory. In the Ceres' frame of reference, the Agnus Dei leaves with the same speed at which it arrives. But when observed in the reference frame of the Solar System, the benefit of this U-turn manoeuvre is obvious. The spacecraft's vector changes as it taps energy from the speed of Ceres orbiting the Sun.

Because the mass of the spacecraft is many orders of magnitude smaller than that of Ceres, while the corresponding result on the Agnus Dei is quite significant, the deceleration reaction experienced by the planet, according to Newton's third law, is utterly imperceptible, so I'm getting a free turnaround without significant loss of speed.

SpaceNav could crunch the numbers on this and provide a hyperbolic path, which means the Agnus Dei can leave Ceres facing in the opposite direction without firing its engine. And, yes, keep its full momentum. I was reassured that SpaceNav was drawing on plenty of examples of previous missions which had used this effect to steer their craft.

Then, a spanner in the works. The angular velocity of the turn meant we'd be pulling Big Gs. Gravity. Not just a few G, but up to 30G according to SpaceNav. Every warning message flashed onto the screen and I had to ask SpaceNav to make the manoeuvre human-safe. SpaceNav dialled everything back and extended the manoeuvre into eight individual short turns, adding in some G-Force offsetting power bursts, to keep the main stresses down to around 8G. It was like the curved sides on one of those British coins. I'd have to get back into the LifePod to protect myself from the forces, but I'd be certain to keep it set to manual operation.

I could program the whole thing into the control deck and then have nearly two months to brood over what could go wrong. But I was going to stay in the moment.

Alone

You have to remember that I'm alone for most of this.

I'm about to attempt one of the most complex space manoeuvres on record and I'm reliant on a SpaceNav system to give me the right instructions. Oh, and there's a tin box full of sheep brains running the other occupants of the space craft.

With a couple of months to wait, I thought I'd tap into their collective conscious before I reply to Cindy.

I use the RightComm to access the Pilot, John Alton. Wow. He is what I'd consider to be a straight-line thinker. Entirely focussed on the Mission. Almost unaware that he's been transferred into another organism. If ever there was a Mister Command Line, then this would be John Alton. I flash up his picture. Cropped haircut, square jaw. Like a toy Action Man figurine. But now, entirely unresisting from his current situation.

Then I try Charlotte Ridley again, our mission specialist. She is the one who was able to first tell me about Lekton and seems to still possess some self-awareness. This time she tells me that her RightMind is becoming more embedded. She is losing her own memories and can tell that they are being substituted by those of her RightMind host.

"This is my truth, now tell me yours," she says, echoing philosophers and politicians back to Nietzsche. All absolutes belong to pathology.

I'm worried that too much exposure to the RightComm link will erode my own mind. I try Carmen Chang-Baez, our international Mission Specialist. She is listening to music, like the first time I tuned in to her RightComm. I recognise "I will follow you into the dark," and realise Carmen has bought the whole programme.

She pauses the music and speaks, "Sam, I have seen dark hours in my life, and I have seen the darkness gradually disappearing, and the light gradually increasing. One by one, I have seen obstacles removed, errors corrected, prejudices softened, proscriptions relinquished, and my advance in all the elements that make up the sum of general welfare. And I remember that whatever delays, disappointments, and discouragements may come, truth, justice, liberty, and humanity will ultimately prevail."

It's a manifesto, riffing on abolitionist Frederick Douglass. I'm guessing it is at the outer limit of what a sheep brain can emulate.

Even the gnarly dude Walter Daimler. He's badged up as a USAF Spaceflight Participant, but I'm still wondering if he's really from some clandestine part of the US Government. I jack into his system. His memories briefly flash up "Stargate," which I realise is an old US-Government project run by the CIA. Most of our crew had suspected Walter as a plant on our mission and now here was evidence which could support it. But Walter gets a hold of my mind almost immediately.

"Charlotte is right," he starts to say. "There's a whole lot happening inside the BrainCore. We all are linked, except you, Sam. And Lekton is trying to manipulate us.

"The Mining Engineers were first to go. All of them. Then your buddies James and Degife. Holly and Carmen held out for a while, but Lekton was purposeful and simply waited. Waited like time didn't matter to him.

"He's added them by now. That's left Charlotte and me. I can use a few of my MK-ULTRA tricks to run interference across Lekton. This he knows and luckily my own brain is a bit scrambled from the copious quantities of psychotropic drugs I ingested during the Gondola Wish and Grill Flame Programs at Fort Meade. It's been enough to provide some psychic cover for Charlotte, but Lekton is still using time as a weapon. My ability to stave off Lekton has maybe another month."

I suddenly realised. Ian Fripp, James Andersen, Degife Abera Bekele, Holly Rider, Carmen Chang-Baez, Byron Abraxas, Peter Geissler, Ulf Dieterssen, Ingmar Skipton, Ilana Skeeter, Christa Zolinskaya. They had all succumbed to both a LifePod Switch and now to a neural grab by Lekton. Walter Daimler was holding out and protecting Charlotte Ridley, but only for another 30 days. I'd only escaped because of my use of the RightMind Manual Control.

I unplug. It is truly like a weight off my mind. I realise Lekton had been gently squeezing down on my still functional brain. I briefly wonder about my surrogate persona running inside the 16-way tin box. Another version of me, only simpler.

I need to tell Cindy.

Rogue

"Cindy calling. Mission Control Earth wants you to continue the mission."

The sound of Cindy's voice overrode everything else on the craft.

"I brought someone else along. It's Lucy."

Cindy had excelled. Not only had she worked out that I was in a difficult situation, but she had also determined that a full human - not an android copy - might be better to help me resolve this. Cindy knew that Lucy could cut the narrative right down to the highlights.

"Hey to both of you. This whole Mission has gone crazily wrong. The entire crew, except for me, is switched into the BrainCore processor. I've tried to communicate with them via RightComm but they are locked down in the XTend."

"There is more to it," answered Lucy, bypassing a response from Cindy "There's a press story developing here on Earth. Mission Control wants the situation to run positive.

"Several ships have already arrived at Ganymede. They are already deploying the mining equipment. Everything is working according to plan. You are 5th in a sequence of ships. Four are deploying successfully and four more after you will be adding greater magnetite mining capability. And that's just from Amerika. Add in Sino-Nihon and Eurussia and Earth has made a big claim towards Ganymede and a mining frontier. It can literally save our planet."

"But what if some systems go rogue?" I ask.

"You are on the only rogue ship. Something happened and they are saying stray malware entered your operation."

"So, what will happen to the ship?" I ask.

"We will run a press story about how you attempt to save it," answers Cindy.

"Attempt?" I ask. 'Attempt' doesn't sound as if it has a happy ending.

"Cindy is leaving out the part where the ship self-destructs in around 40 days," answers Lucy.

"Could this be terrorism?" I ask, "Or some kind of industrial espionage?"

"We've run all the scenarios," answers Cindy. "The only one which computes is a malware leakage."

"Cindy is speaking as a proxy for the entire Mission Control," says Lucy, "It's why they bonded her with you, so that you would trust her."

I realise I'm getting my information supplied via an android mixing console, albeit a beautiful one. Cindy's autonomy has thoughtfully brought along Lucy to provide a line of interpretation.

Lucy adds: "They will want the ship to be visible from Earth when they destroy it - for Social Media and the Press - You will be so much collateral damage."

"What about the XTend? And the appearance of Lekton? He seems so real to Charlotte."

Cindy continues, "Lekton is an aberration. We picked up Lekton from Mission Control. It seems to want to negotiate with us. Something about running an Earth Council."

"Is there such a thing?"

"Not yet, but it is being mooted. Like the Council we proposed for Ganymede. Three main members. Amerika, Sino-Nihon and Eurussia."

"I can see that on Ganymede, it could work. Keep the balance of power even. But on Earth? There are too many vested interests. It goes well beyond the United Nations."

"Exactly. That is Lekton's play. He - or I should say IT - wants to be in change. Like an entity managing the Earth. Ultimate power and all."

"There is a way," says Lucy. "Give Lekton a different target to run against."

"Diversionary?" I ask.

"Play it for real," answers Lucy.

This whole thing is getting crazier by the minute. Now an artificial entity wants control of Earth. Lucy, my human co-conspirator is suggesting that we create a dummy target for Lekton. Something believable that he/it can take over. I can see where this is heading.

"The crew," asks Lucy, "You have them running inside the XTend?"

"Oh yes," I answer, "And I can still communicate through one of them - Charlotte Ridley."

"Tell her, tell her that the crew is about to become a member of Earth Council," says Lucy., "It will be Lekton's lucky day because he already has significant control over the XTend."

I brace myself to go back on-line to the RightMind. I expect to have Lekton onto my head within minutes.

Sure enough, I can still reach Charlotte, although she now seems more distant. I tell her that she and the rest of the crew are to be appointed as Earth Council. Charlotte isn't having any of it, though. She protests that such a move would place this craft and Earth in danger.

I explain that we have seen the balance of probabilities and that this would be best for Earth. I can sense Lekton in the background, like so much smoke drifting across our conversation. There is a small click and the comms to Charlotte increases in clarity. I sense Lekton must be willing this gambit to succeed.

"How will it happen?" asks Charlotte.

"Simple," I answer, passing back Cindy's reply from Mission Control, "You'll receive a token. It will be all you need."

I marvel at how the command chain can be digitised. I guess it does not differ from the symbolism of orbs and sceptres used by Earth's establishment monarchy to confer status and power. Here, the transfer of power will be by a non-fungible token, closely akin to the orb and sceptre, but without the legacy baggage. I'm sure Lekton will be delighted to harvest the token for his own purposes.

"When?" asks Charlotte, suddenly alert.

"Re-dock minus twenty days," I answer.

Things are about to get very lively around the Agnus Dei. I unplug from the RightComm before Lekton can get any closer to me. I'm suddenly back with Cindy's voice on the Agnus Dei.

"Did it work?" asks Cindy. "We have no sense of Lekton here. His links don't work, and we have no other means to monitor anything."

"Yes, it worked," I answer. "Re-dock minus twenty days."

Miracle needed

Our ship, Agnus Dei, is the fifth in line destined for Ganymede. The first four from the Elysium Mission were successful, but then ours was jinxed. My crew of fourteen were correctly in suspended animation on their way to Ganymede when something went wrong with our LifePods. Every one of them has been switched to a backup, which is running from inside the XTend unit.

They are all running as surrogates. Simplified humans, running on sheep's brains. They are all interconnected like a hive mind and Earth is about to pass them control of Earth Council.

Somehow, the ship is also inhabited by an entity called Lekton, which appears to want to take control of the Earth Council.

Meanwhile, Earth's press is building a new narrative for the demise of this Elysium Mission craft. Not when I turn it around, but later when I get close enough to Earth for the inhabitants to see it, like some kind of firework show. We are to be sacrificed when the explosion can be seen from Earth. We become a news story, yet conveniently the problem of the LifePod switch and of Lekton gets buried.

I'll need a miracle to get out of this.

Then Lucy calls.

Lucy's Plan

Lucy calls, "So tomorrow you make the Ceres manoeuvre?"

"Yes - to turn me around and back towards Earth. I'll be travelling at around Mach 30. Fast enough to be an edge condition for a black hole."

"But you are breaking the manoeuvre into smaller parts. Nothing over Mach 8?"

"Correct. I'll be like a series of small juddery turns. Eight in total. I've programmed them into the Agnus Dei."

"Okay, except for one small thing. An amendment to your calculations. It is for turn seven, of eight."

I realise what Lucy is saying. She wants me to change the manoeuvre.

"You'll be creating two vectors on the turn seven. A new one for Agnus Dei, and a different almost undetectable one for Dolly."

Lucy sends me two new vectors. One for me and a

different one for Agnus Dei. I notice that Lucy is also re-routing the main ship, sending it into deep space.

My mind reaches back to the escape vehicle. It was officially Agnus Dei EV-S01, but the crew had anointed it as Dolly and even painted a sheep picture on the hull, like an old warplane would have a buxom woman painted on the side for luck. Dolly was the first of Earth's sheep clones and had been taken to heart by the crew.

Lucy is describing this over free air to me and I can't help wondering whether Lekton can hear what is being discussed.

"We are okay. Lekton uses comms intercept to monitor messaging. Our speech is in a different realm and he won't be able to tap into it," explains Lucy.

I hope so. Now we've a plan to interrupt the last part of the turnaround manoeuvre. If it goes to plan, I'll be sent on one path and the Agnus Dei and its occupants will be going in another direction. I check Lucy's calculations on the SpaceNav.

I will be pointed back toward Moon Two and the Agnus Dei will fire away from Earth, along with its XTend cargo and presumably with Lekton still on board.

The change of direction is subtle and it could take at least three days for it to be discovered as a variance. It will be enough time to put a huge gap between me and the Agnus Dei.

Just as importantly, this all happens before the supposed tragic demise of Agnus Dei, which has been choreographed to occur at T-20 days. In other words, the explosion of the main craft would have been visible to a naked eye from Earth. I guess that Earth must send the destruct signal, but now that the Agnus Dei has been rerouted, it will be too far away for such a signal to function.

Now, with Lucy's adaptation of the manoeuvre, I can no longer predict what will happen.

Fairground Ride

The next day, it is Cindy who breaks into the comms on the Agnus Dei. I was expecting Lucy, but Cindy explains something to me.

"Affinity."

"What?"

"Affinity. You and I have great affinity. It will serve us both well in later stages."

I don't know what Cindy is taking about.

"You realised? At least I assume you realised?"

"Realised what?"

"That you have been patched, Maybe only 1% but you still have some cyborg componentry."

I do not know what Cindy is taking about. There is a bleep on the comms.

"I'm not supposed to ever tell you that, but I guess this is a moment for truth - as we start the manoeuvre," she adds.

"You and I were paired together. Cindy Shaw and Sam Walker. We were supposed to be Primes, not space crew. If we bring you back, it will be to resume your Prime function, here on Earth, or maybe on Moon Two."

I reel from this knowledge. I don't feel any different, but I realise I must be.

"How?" I ask.

"You were a reclaim from an auto accident, just like me. You have been patched, although only in the very slightest manner, by Brant Industries. Just enough to make you a suitable candidate for pairing. I thought you would realise when you ran into Kendle, back when Lucy was showing you around the lab."

"Kendle? The stand-alone unit."

"Yes, one of many similar units which has a default persona. It's what Brant will do to protect you. You know, from the effects of Lekton and so-on."

"What? I'll be reset?" I ask. There are too many new facts emerging all at once.

A warble sounds.

"It's time," says Cindy. "The first of the space manoeuvres. You should climb into the safety capsule - into Dolly - to avoid the huge turning forces."

I scramble into the escape pod – which looks to me like an adapted LifePod but can be separated from the main craft. I make sure that everything is set to Manual. As I settle into the escape pod, everything shakes and I realise we are entering the first manoeuvre.

It is also when I realise that I'd programmed the manoeuvres based directly on the SpaceNav. Instead of leaving a timed gap between the first manoeuvre and the second, I've somehow managed to make them run into one another. I'm counting and we are already on manoeuvre 3. It's like an over-zealous fairground ride. Scream if you want to go faster.

Through the judders I can see the capsule is displaying a countdown sequence for me. Five manoeuvres complete, now three still to run. I feel as if I've been rolling on a continuous wave machine for the last ten minutes. Now we are approaching the end of the sequence and I can see we have turned around. This is when the extra programming suggested by Lucy will cut in.

The rescue pod warbles and a new red light comes on. Never a good sign although before I have any time to react, I hear explosive bolts detaching the rescue pod and a significant smaller space craft from the rest of the Agnus Dei.

There's a crash and then a boom, which somehow overrides the silence of space. I realise it is all mechanics and I'm being transmitted vibrations along the spacecraft hull.

A final punch of defiant acceleration, and I realise that my pod – Dolly - attached to a sizeable space cruiser is now reaching out into space. Below me, I can see the massive glittering shape of Agnus Dei, setting its new course vector away from me. We are travelling 15 degrees apart and counterintuitively it looks as if the

Agnus Dei still has the distinct speed advantage and is falling away from me.

'Vector 45, separation,' chimes the SpaceNav. 'Pre-programmed manoeuvre completed. Main craft now running with an argument of periapsis vectoring toward the Sun.'

The Agnus Dei is on a collision course for the sun. I see its booster rockets firing in sequence. It is attempting to careen its way out of the current course. Something else has taken control – I'm guessing it is Lekton or maybe the crew if they have been awoken in the XTend.

I check for any adjustments to my own course, but as far as I can tell I am still aimed for Moon Two, on a rapidly decelerating space craft.

The radio cuts in. It is Cindy, "Manoeuvre completed. You have detached from the main spacecraft and are now in the rescue module, still contained within the EV-S01 rescue pod."

"What about Lekton?" I ask.

"Still attached to the Agnus Dei. Lekton has now acquired the fifteen crew members completely and is repurposing them for control of Earth Council."

Bartering Chips

Things have stabilised. The Agnus Dei has gone, it is on a routing toward the sun, but appears to be trying to wriggle its way out of its current setting. My rescue craft has slowed down and is positioning for what looks like a docking manoeuvre with Moon Two.

A failed earth politician once tried to make a speech about taking back control. He failed entirely, and it is roughly how I'm feeling now, with the EV-S01 safety pod now making its own orbital adjustments, ready of a manoeuvre which will see me re-dock with Earth Two.

I do not know where Agnus Dei has gone, with its tragic cargo of crew, which have now been hijacked by Lekton as so many bartering chips to admit him to Earth Council.

Cindy's voice cuts through.

"I'm with Lucy. Sam, we'll make sure you get back to Moon Two safely. Everything is going to plan."

I realise I'm also a mere cog in some grand scheme and that Cindy's voice represents Mission Control but packaged up as some form of reassurance.

I need to talk to Lucy and ask for her directly in the

comms unit. I need to negotiate my persistence, not a reprogramming reset.

"It's simple enough," I say. "I know the moves now. I've seen it all. I should be kept in my current state, with the knowledge I already have. Resetting me will simply endanger everyone else. New crews won't be any the wiser about what happened, nor know about any more stray Lektons interfering with the crew and cargo. I can assist, but only if I'm allowed to maintain my current instance."

There is a long pause. I know that Mission Control is discussing my wish. They know they have something unique and should question whether the best thing is to nullify it.

Cindy responds.

"Mission Control agrees with your diagnosis. One thing though. They want to keep you Earthside, not on the next space mission. You can be vigilant over multiple craft this way. I have already been designated as a Prime and you would be my counterpart, set up on a base which is Earthside or on Moon Two."

I think about this for a moment. It seems like a useful compromise and won't limit my future actions.

"And what about Lucy?" I ask.

A man's voice answers, "You have already gained her as support crew to you two as Primes. She stays."

This is good news, as long as it is reliable.

"You will have to go through some minor reality

adjustment on Moon Two. Nothing drastic, but we need to synchronise your version of reality," explains the Mission, "It will be mainly to eliminate ghosting from what has just happened."

Ghosting. The removal of shadow artefacts that could trip me into a different reality because of what I know. I remember this from IPX training. A kind of repainting of the background scenery.

"Okay, It's fine, but no funny business?" I question.

"No, you are more valuable to use paired with Cindy and installed on Moon Two," answered the Mission. I realise I must now be talking directly to the Mission Controller.

Mendacious Backstories

I reach the edge of Earth's space. I'm close enough to pick up news broadcasts and to use normal comms for P2P/Person to Person conversations.

There's a common story running around about the demise of Agnus Dei, the fifth Elysium SkyTrain Mission aimed toward Ganymede, but the only one of a series of ten ships which has run into any kind of difficulty.

The press story runs that Agnus Dei carried an experimental type of computer processor and that it failed through overheating soon after take-off. It was an entirely made-up story and mentioned nothing about the crew being switched to the XTend, nor of the discovery and influence of Lekton.

The stories also described how the entire brave crew had fought to regain control of the ship, but once its navigation was destroyed, they had no choice but to follow a pre-defined path toward the sun. This differed from the story I'd been told earlier in the Mission. It seemed like the story needed its own damage limitation.

I could read my own obituary backstory including my

fictional Catholic schooling as vicious as any Roman rule. My memory told me how my knuckles were bruised by a lady in black and how I held my tongue as she told me, 'Son, fear is the heart of love.' Spurious detail to aid realism.

They were using guilt and darkness to manipulate my profile. They didn't realise how ineffective it was when I was not being processed by RightMind. I noticed that my self-awareness was even heightened.

The press was having a field day, safe knowing that there could be no-one to refute any of the stories. They clearly didn't know about me travelling earthwards on a separate trajectory.

And I knew there were no blinding lights or tunnels to gates of white. My real brain was still functioning, although I was all too well aware that its persistence was in the hands of Cindy and Lucy.

PART FOUR - VEDANTA

तत्त्व

Tattva, achintya bheda abheda tattva
Tattva, achintya bheda abheda tattva
Tattva, achintya bheda abheda tattva
Tattva, achintya bheda abheda tattva

Like the flower and the scent of summer
Like the sun and the shine
Well, the truth may come in strange disguises
Send a message to your mind

At the moment that you wake from sleeping
And you know it's all a dream
Well, the truth may come in strange disguises
Never knowing what it means

For you shall be tomorrow
Like you have been today
If this was never ending
What more can you say?

Crispian Mills

Between two and five

Earthside, there is that time between around two in the morning and five in the morning when everything seems to speed up. Maybe the brain is partly asleep and downplays the rush of time? I don't know, but anyway, I experienced a similar effect on the last days leading back to Moon Two.

I had expected it to be a long, drawn-out experience. There was no time for ennui. Instead, the discipline of daily procedures on my small craft. That, and the knowledge that at the end of it all, I would have to gently land in a tiny docking bay. I'd have travelled some 120 million kilometres from earth and back. Yet it would all be down to a successful landing in the last 1000 metres.

All the time, there is a large green button on the rescue console. It says one word on it.

Dock.

I've checked the manual, and it seems to be an automated procedure for re-docking. It says to press the innocuous-looking control button when speeding inbound 190 kilometres from Moon Two.

I wonder how reliable a button is, which has probably never been field tested. It's a button on the escape capsule from a massive space craft. I'm approaching 190 kilometres from Moon Two. That's about 15 earth diameters distant from our docking point.

I press the button.

Dock.

Instantly, all the engines fire. I feel huge deceleration. A voice system says 'positioning', like some kind of robot vacuum cleaner. The craft rotates, as if calibrating its whereabouts. A map display appears on the HUD.

'Head Up Display activated and aligning' says a disembodied voice. I notice a slight French accent and then remember that the escape capsule was made in Switzerland by Brant Industry.

'aligné,' says the French voice. This does not give me great confidence. How could they have given me a French language capsule? This part has never been tested.

'début de l'amarrage,' says the system. I now notice on the display a button shaped like a cog. I assume it is the settings control, but I'm too nervous to press it mid-manoeuvre.

Then suddenly, we've closed the gap from 15 earth diameters to less than one. At what, to me, seems like an alarming speed, we make our way into the docking bay and then automatically fire retro stabilisers. There are small adjustments as we align perfectly with the bay and then a resonant thump as I realise we have docked.

'nous sommes amarrés'. 'We are docked,' says the tenuously bi-lingual control system. I check for atmosphere inside Dolly and then cautiously open the capsule. I can immediately taste the difference. Freshly scrubbed and filtered air contrasts with the thousands of times recycled air in my escape pod.

But I don't care. I've made it to Moon Two and can still walk. I climb from the pod just as I notice four military types in bright yellow armour walking toward me. There is really no need for them to be carrying weapons.

Come with us

I was always warned about 'come with us' style assertions. 'Please step into the vehicle', 'everything will be fine, now', 'safe and secure', 'this is for your own good,' – Well, it was just about to happen to me.

"Welcome to Moon Two. You'll need to come with us," says the man in command, "To the Medical Facility."

I look around. I realise that I'm alone with the four yellow military types. That Cindy isn't with me. I have to keep reminding myself that I'm back from my RightMind dream.

At least I think I am.

Then I hear Cindy's voice - it is like she has jumped from the RightDream, but I realise that she is on the comms system.

"Hey, stranger! Welcome back - I guess you will be somewhat disorientated?"

Something sounds off. Cindy isn't speaking to me in her

normal manner. I guess it is a synth. I'm listening to a Cindy voice being run through a synthesiser. Before I have time to test my theory, she says something else.

"Sam, I've got Lucy here with me."

Now the difference between Cindy and Lucy was one of degree. Cindy had the words but seldom said anything I'd regard as personal. Lucy was bursting with personal stories and - well - emotion. But both these voices both sounded real.

I try my test.

"Lucy, remember that time when my favorite colors were pink and green?" I ask. Lucy would know that line from one of her favourite songs. She'd also know the next one.

A pause. "Don't be silly," answers Lucy, "Your favourite colour is Red!"

Wrong answer, Lucybot. I'm talking to a pair of synths. Keep up, Control, read the footnotes.

"Hey, remember that time when my favorite colors were pink and green?
Hey, remember that month when I only ate boxes of tangerines?
So cheap and juicy"

I decide to try something else.

"Charlotte told me," I say, "When she was in the LifePod."

"Told you what?" asks Cindybot.

"Told me about the Switch. That everyone was switched

into the BrainCore," I use 'The Switch' as the Mission euphemism for the crew being flipped into sheep's brains and put on 'brain support'.

"Exactly. That is why we want to talk to you further. To understand what happened on the ship to cause the Switch."

I can sense the four yellow armoured men have formed a square around me.

I answer, "Nothing happened, as far as I could tell. No-one on the ship touched anything. But all the LifePods had Red warning lights. I reset them to Blue status easily enough."

"Exactly. Blue means they were operating through the BrainCore. That their consciousness had been transferred via XTend."

"Yes, and they seemed to acquire a hive mind too?"

"Exactly. That was always part of the design. You realise there is a parallel version of you, Sam Walker, running inside of BrainCore?"

It hadn't occurred to me. I wonder whether the 'other me' is freaking out at the moment inside the XTend's BrainCore. I know I'm close to losing it myself.

"What about Lekton?" I ask. Try to find out what is really happening.

"Lekton? You saw Lekton?" asks Cindy's voice.

"No, I didn't, but Charlotte did."

"How?"

The voice responses are getting shorter. I guess I'm into uncharted territory.

"Charlotte told me that Lekton was on the Agnus Dei."

"Did she see him?"

"No. She felt him. Lekton inhabited the ship and then ran a remote shutdown. I escaped because my LifePod was set to Manual. Everyone else was switched to the secondary system inside the XTend box."

I remember that feeling of something spider-like passing over my head. I could almost feel it now but realise it must be my imagination.

I decide to tell them. Offer some information and see whether they will give anything back.

After I describe the encounter with Lekton, a man's voice came onto the comms.

"Sam, you have brushed against Lekton. Few live to give such an account. My name is Kjeld Nikolajsen and I work in Brant labs. We have been developing RightMind over many years, first as individual units and then as composites, run on organic brains, supplemented with digital technology."

I realise immediately that Brant's interest must be military. Embed combat troop intelligence within individual weapons. Super-connect the hive mind and augment it with digital smarts. Brant had miscalculated - this was not just of military importance; it was toxically political too. No wonder Lekton was interested.

The armed yellow men edge even closer as I realise, I'm an accidental key-holder for dark secrets.

"Here's the deal," says Kjeld Nikolajsen. "There's two ways we can run this."

"First - I can ask these four gentlemen to acquire your mind. To simply add you to our RightMind collection."

"Why would you do that?" I ask, playing for time.

"Simple. We don't want you spreading news about Brant nor how far we have got with development of the RightMind."

"And the other option?" I ask.

"This was Cindy's idea. She asks that you and she be allowed to resume roles inside the Elysium Mission, although it would be at a different point in its history. You would be two Primes, on Earth, working with people installed on Ganymede."

I can see that option has an upside, but I wonder whether there is any downside.

"What's the catch?" I ask.

"Simply that we have to reprocess you. Remove any vestiges of pre-knowledge. Remove ghosting from your RealDream. Remove your advance knowledge of Lekton. You'll have to discover everything as it unfolds."

I wonder if Kjeld is for real. The second option seems much better than the first one.

A blue arc cuts across the room. It reminds me of the ribbon ray I saw when they were hunting for Sven. Out from it steps Cindy.

"You'd be working with me, " she says, "And yes, I'm the real person who you knew from IPX."

"And Lucy?" I ask.

"She is not on your timeline," says Kjeld, " You will forget you ever knew her."

Cindy smiles and beckons for me to go into the next room. I can see it has been set up with a sleek, modern version of RightMind. Cindy encourages me to place the RightMind headgear on my head.

"What about the BrainCore?" I ask., "The rest of the crew?"

"Nothing to worry about. They are on still on a Mission, with Lekton. He is trying to run a deal to become part of Earth Council's Senate."

Cindy has clipped the RightMind to my head and powers it on. "Just go with the feeling and you'll be back in next to no time. Back properly with me. Sam Walker, your time will come."

I suddenly feel tired. I'm sure I'm being manipulated followed by a long sensation of falling.

Ed Adams

Earthside

Now I'm watching someone named Roeloff. I've dialled into his Streamcom.

I hear his apartment judder. A mournful sigh. This one had been close, but not that close. I know his building is designed for it.

Then I see Roeloff look towards the window. Grey night skies, something resembling clouds, thin trails, raked towards the horizon.

I look at the clock. Ten minutes to midnight. This would go on until the morning. More crashes and thumps as the battering continues.

If Roeloff can stay inside, he can watch some transmissions to take his mind off the situation.

I watch Roeloff move from his bedroom into the main living area. He flips a switch and suddenly I can hear the weather. A gentle rain and a rustling of leaves. The occasional spatter of water dripping from branches. Roeloff keeps his weather set to April. Outside it was the end of summer but somehow it did not matter what the official calendar said, Roeloff decides he will run it at his own speed.

I watch Roeloff flip the screen. Not the full screen but the one designed to show just entertainment transmissions and data. It opens on a standard news transmission and he gestures for it to move across to his messages.

His main room has noise cancellation and so I am no longer aware of the crashes from outside.

I recognise this scene with a sense that I've been here before. The RightDream I've been in has clearly messed with my mind.

"Peter give me status," Roeloff asks.

A small pop-up window appears on the top right of the screencom. Everything is green. At this rate, there will be nothing to do.

I watch Roeloff walk across to the kitchen area, flip a tap, and drink some water. The tap illuminates the water as it pours. The blue colour signifies that the source is both pure and cold. It all seems so real.

A little information light on the screen briefly flickers to amber. A moment later it returns to green.

"Hi Peter," Roeloff requests, "please provide an update on base status."

"Full base status is green. There was a short incident with a meteorite, but a rail gun cleared it. Incident duration 1.2 seconds. There are zero requests for your attendance at the base."

Roeloff walks to the kitchen cupboard and flips open a compartment.

"Peter, dispense modafinil. Two units."

Two small capsules appear in the compartment. I watch Roeloff place them in his mouth and take a small drink from the water glass. I can see Roeloff react to the rush. Senses heightened as if he had been over-clocked like a computer.

The modafinil was for mission use. Roeloff had someone fix Peter's system so that there was always a modest threat level running. In these conditions, Peter would unquestioningly dispense the drugs. The same system fix meant that Peter also lost track of how many drugs were dispensed.

Roeloff just needed to remember not to get the automatic updates for the health-care system in the apartment. That was another advantage of being off base. Living quarters on the base would always run with the latest and greatest versions of everything.

A chime sounded from the streamcom. "Peter accept," Roeloff says.

A small repeater screen in the kitchen shows the faces of colleagues.

"Hi Roelof, it's Jasmijn. There's something very unusual happening here. The incoming shower seems to be concentrated on our control centre. We've already lost the above-ground units and now the incoming is creating a crater where the underground centre is located. At this rate, we'll have lost everything within another 15 minutes."

"What about the HSDA?" asks Roelof.

"I know. This is one time where our fast reflex friends should be able to solve this without us even noticing. I've seen the high-speed defence array running today almost non-stop. There's no question it's been working, but it just doesn't seem to be enough to stop this. It's almost as if the meteors have their own avoidance telemetry."

"Do I need to come in?" asks Roelof.

"I don't think you would be in time to make any difference," says Jasmijn. "We are all being backed into a corner here. They've already given the order to flip command to another centre."

Peter interrupted the transmission, "I am stabilising the display. It exceeds my tolerance levels."

"Hi Peter, remove video stabilisation," requests Roelof.

I can see Jasmijn on Roeloff's display as the stabilisation is removed. Shaky doesn't describe it. The base was designed to withstand just about anything that could be thrown at it. Quakes, powerful winds, floods, fire. The original designers had borrowed the triple X symbol from the Earthside town of Amsterdam. Fire flood and pestilence. Three Xs. Three times "No".

Triple X Protection.

Jasmijn looked back towards the camera. "I'm gonna bail," she says. "I'm guessing this place is only going to be around for a few more minutes."

He heard the noise of a siren. Then a bleep and the

screen terminates.

"Transmission terminated," says Peter.

"Peter, please give me externals," requests Roelof, "Put it on the main wall."

He steps back into the living space. All across the wall is a scene showing distant clouds, a red sky, and white streaks of light focused on a smoking central area.

Roelof walks to a console in the living space. He sits in a swivel chair and grabs the controls. He looks around the sky and locks on to two monitor drones.

Requesting access to their video channels, he zooms the drones towards the distant control centre. The external centre disappears and then that an ominous hole in the ground suggests the Secondary bunker was also compromised.

"Jasmijn, Jasmijn, do you copy?"

Roeloff repeats the request a couple more times.

Then a voice. "Copy that, Jasmijn here - I can hear you."

" What is your status?"

" The pod is secure, and I am outside the main ring of damage. Another 20 seconds and it would be very different. It looks as if some of the others have made it too."

"Okay, follow the protocol and join me here," says Roelof.

"Copy that,"

Roeloff's apartment complex had been designed to protect as many people as possible on the base. Everyone had been paired, and Roeloff had been selected to pair with Jasmijn. He was officially English, and she was officially Belgian, although neither of them had spent much time in their designated home countries.

I watch as Roelof flicks through some of the observation systems to check the wider impacts of what had happened. This was one of the worst storms seen since Roeloff had been active on Ganymede. There was also something very unusual about the focus of this storm. Usually, anything that appeared in the weather systems was quite predictable in the way that it travelled across the winds of the surface. Although violent, the normal storms dissipated across large geographical tracts. This protected the mines and other constructions from acute damage.

A paradox was that the very substances wanted from Ganymede and the adjacent Europa for use on Earth could also be harnessed within Ganymede's own biosphere.

For around two hundred years, the magnetosphere of Jupiter's largest moon had been observable from Earth. It had only been for the last 40 years that dependable space transit had been possible. The discovery of two complimentary passive minerals that, when combined, created a magnetic field like that within an electricity generator had been a breakthrough discovery.

Small amounts of the minerals could make powerful generators which could be used for domestic and commercial purposes back on Earth. The same technology could be used in situ on Ganymede to create the required defence shields to protect the mining and other operations from danger. For planet Earth, this had been a life-saving discovery such that as fossil fuels declined, the new availability of magnetite had become a complete game-changer.

Now I realise that I'm replaying parts of RightDream's context, except this is supposedly happening now.

The original predictions of a six-year flight from Earth had been dramatically reduced to three years in each direction, augmented with the creation of SkyTrains to provide a near continuous round-trip service. For a two-year stay on Ganymede base, there was the prospect of considerable wealth for those that pioneered the creation and exploration of the bases.

The sovereign structure of Ganymede had been incorporated into Earth's United Nations although a series of different and sometimes very unconventional procedures had been allowed. The Earth Council superseded the United Nations, although the exact sequence of events and their timing was hazy.

The jurisdiction was not so much 'out of sight, out of mind' as a series of procedures to support the necessities of developing a base to support the future of humankind so far from Earth.

Pioneers to Ganymede had taken the longer and slower six-year outbound trip, then two or so years working and then the faster three-year return cycle using newer technology driven by Ganymede's own propulsion devices.

I know this includes the failed flight of Agnus Dei as part

of the Elysium Mission.

In practical terms, the round trip equals an 11-year absence. During that time, the first settlers created the capabilities for mining to be successful. The round-trip with work time was now reduced to eight years. Three outbound, two on Ganymede and then three to return.

Most people on earth were unaware of change taking place on Ganymede. It was much further than a distant small country and as long as the requisite technologies arrived in time to be useful than the main debates were about the rise in fortunes of those that had made the return trip.

I knew that Roelof and Jasmijn knew little about the situation on earth. There were some individuals, sometimes referred to as the Sharps, who seemed to have a much better knowledge of life on Earth. Curiously, the Sharps were perceived by people like Roelof and Jasmijn as dim-witted and slow thinking.

The buzzer to Roelof's landing deck signalled the arrival of Jasmijn.

"Peter, please guide her in."

"Acknowledged," responds Peter.

A few minutes later, Jasmijn buzzes again, and Peter opens the main door to the apartment.

"Are you okay?" asks Roelof.

"Everything is fine," says Jasmijn. "That was a close thing, but I think most of us evacuated each area before it was destroyed."

"It's still a very worrying change of situation," says Roelof, "It's the worst I remember, after nearly two years and despite the hostile environment, there has been nothing like this."

At that moment, Peter interrupts, "I have an incoming transmission for both of you."

"Okay, Peter, put it on the wall."

A newsflash appears on the living space wall. It is accompanied by newscaster soundtrack music. Then a flash and both Roelof and Jasmijn momentarily tip their heads sideways. Four seconds later, the news broadcast resumes with a good news story from Perth about a pet dog found after it had run away from home.

"Okay then," says Roelof to Jasmijn. "I'll meet you at the alternate control centre tomorrow."

"That's fine," says Jasmijn, as she leaves the apartment.

I realise I'll need to learn fast.

The next book in this Edge series…

| Edge | World end climate collapse and sham discovered during magnetite mining from Jupiter's moon Ganymede. | https://amzn.to/2KDmYOW |

Sheep Dreams

Sheep Dreams

Ed Adams

www.ingramcontent.com/pod-product-compliance
Lightning Source LLC
Chambersburg PA
CBHW060926120626
46557CB00003B/886